TOUCHING HARRY

Other work by Peter Robins includes

Short Stories
    Undo Your Raincoats And Laugh
    Our Hero Has Bad Breath
    The Gay Touch (U.S.A.)
    Summer Shorts

Novels
    Easy Stages
    Survivors

Edited
    Doves For The Seventies
    Oranges And Lemons
    The Freezer Counter (September 1989)

TOUCHING HARRY

Peter Robins

THIRD HOUSE (Publishers)

First published in April 1989 by Third House (Publishers)
35 Brighton Road, London N16 8EQ, England

World copyright © Peter Robins 1989

ISBN 1 870188 098

Photoset by Rapid Communications Ltd,
27 Swinton Street, London WC1

Printed and bound by Billing & Sons Ltd, Worcester

Distributed in Europe by Turnaround,
27 Horsell Road, London N5 1XL

Cover design by Rupert Kirby.
Cover painting by Alain Roselló.

for Robin Houston

Harry pushes his exercise book away. He has completed one paragraph of an essay and even that does not satisfy him. Without enthusiasm, he glances again at the slip of paper handed to him at the end of his Civics lesson.

There is no case for a major post-war plan in this borough. The restoration of such worthwhile property as has been damaged by bombing will suffice together with the construction of one new council estate on the site of the former sewage works. Discuss.

It occurs to Harry that this theme could well have been suggested by his Uncle Cliff or any of his Aunt Winifred's Town Hall cronies. To agree with it would be to acquiesce in providing all the estate agents and builders' merchants on the Council with a carte blanche that would fatten even further their already sleek bank balances.

Yet to disagree entailed arguing a case. This he is unable to do. Preoccupied with the need to discuss his future with his parents – whatever the emotional cost – he is incapable of shaping his thoughts on town planning into any presentable order. He fiddles with his fountain pen and peers – first at John and then Margaret – from under his mop of hair.

Accepting that he'll not be able to concentrate on any vision of a new and more equitable world until his own future has taken a step forward, he pushes back his hair, gulps and addresses his parents.

–The Headmaster talked to all of us in the Sixth this afternoon. We each had to say what we intend to do when we leave next July.

Harry waits for some reaction to this. So does Margaret Plimsoll. John Leonard Plimsoll – descendant of South Devon farmers – continues to stroke the neck of the cat at his feet. Does he notice that his wife glances at him over the rims of her reading glasses? It would appear not. Harry suspects his father may no longer need to check such a routine gesture. It is also possible that John Plimsoll has a private bet on how long it will be before Margaret sighs and rests her knitting on her lap. Harry counts ten seconds before she does so.

–If you're hinting that Dr Garstone was trying to discover which of the Forces you intend to join, I trust you told him the R.A.F. Even you – self-centred as you are – might have observed that they're just a little above the run of the common soldiery. In any event, it'll all be over before you're eighteen. When I was queuing for dried bananas this morning I was told that Monty had been seen leaving Kneller Hall again. On his way to meet Ike, no doubt. There'll be a second front in the spring and that'll be it. So there's no point in your talking about being called up. . .

–Isn't that a rather selfish way of looking at it, my dear? After all. . .

–After all, John, I've given three nephews already. Dunkirk . . . Narvik . . . Tobruk. . .

Waiting for the recital to conclude, Harry again runs his hand through his hair. When his father makes no reply – fumbling, instead, for a Craven A – Harry realises he must press on with what will be perceived as resolution.

–Well, you see, that wasn't what we were being asked. The Old Man already knew who was in the Air Training Corps and which of us are Messenger Boys at the Town Hall. . .

He falters into silence. Knowing that it will not happen, that their past indifference will not miraculously give way to enthusiasm or even interest, Harry leaves the next move to his parents. John clears his throat and assumes the unhappy look of one compelled to speak under duress.

–Well then? . . . Out with it . . . What's all the mystery?

–There's no mystery, Father.

–Well then, damnit . . . What did you say you intended to do next year?

10

–There just wasn't anything I've always wanted to do that I felt I could mention. . .

Harry falters once more. This is partly attributable to Margaret's reaction. Her son is slightly unnerved that she should resume her knitting. He calculates that it must be tea-cosy number sixteen. He stares at the plum-red wool, suspecting it to be the left-overs of a jersey he has outgrown. He wonders how she can consider the need to finish more of the wretched objects in time for one of Winifred's Aid To Something Or Other Bazaars more vital than anything her only child is about to reveal of his intentions. Harry feels she has knitted his future long since and now dispassionately awaits the moment to slip it over his shoulders – a larger and more durable jersey.

–That's all very well, Harry. Surely you must have given Dr Garstone some inkling. . . ?

–Well. . .

Margaret Plimsoll, née McCawdie, barely pauses as she counts her rows of stitches.

–Inkling, fiddlesticks. You know very well your father and I would have wished you to become a chartered accountant. Since your Maths results were appalling and you've chosen to study Arts or whatever you call it, you'd better find something practical you can do with all this poetry and theatricals. For the life of me I can't think what. . .

Tightening his lips, Harry looks down at the cat. The animal is – in strategic terms – a neutral zone. An overfed Sweden or Switzerland carrying no one's flags or pennants in its fur. Harry wonders whether he should mention that he's just noticed the creature has fleas. Aware that this would be a diversionary tactic, he reproaches himself. John Plimsoll has started to hum some tuneless air. Every member of the Plimsoll family knows this to be an amber warning – the prelude to some outburst of irritation. As the cat stretches, Harry notices that his father is staring at him.

–Let's just hope you didn't make a laughing-stock of yourself in front of your school-mates. This writing nonsense I'm referring to. What Dr Garstone would make of this poetry lark I'm sure I don't know. As for the acting business, I just pray that's all over and done with. . .

The wariness with which Harry promoted this skirmish hasn't been forgotten. It's no moment for pointing to a flaw in his father's reasoning. To dismiss actors as dissolute and impoverished in one breath and then, some million breaths later, to express admiration for a brother-in-law who'd chucked over a clerical pittance to become a walk-on at Pinewood Studios might be contradictory but Harry knows better than to mention it.

Naif he might be but Harry Plimsoll is no fool. His incautious enthusiasms have resulted in bruises. He lacks the guile of the ambitious yet, slowly, and not the easy way, he's learning the basics of self-protection. Conse-uently, there have been no major domestic explosions for a couple of months – since his announcement that his work as a Civil Defence Messenger at the Town Hall would entail night duties. He takes care now to avoid any repetition of that bloodily-won victory.

–I didn't mention poetry or acting, Father.

–That's a mercy. So, are we to hear what you did say, or do your mother and I have to wait until the nine o'clock news is over?

–Well, I had to offer something to shut the Old Man up. I said I had thought of becoming a teacher. . .

John Plimsoll sucks at a hollow tooth as he stares, unblinking, at his son. Margaret looks once more over the rims of her glasses but only to inspect the finished tea-cosy which she begins to plump up with tissue paper. She feels no need to pre-empt her husband's reaction.

–I'm speechless, Harry. Speechless. What did your Head-master say?

–He's asked me to go and see him in the morning.

As Margaret begins to laugh, Harry discovers that he can – for the first time – watch this performance without dropping his gaze. Even more satisfying is the realisation that he is progressively less wounded by her derision.

If he were asked for the exact date when her opinion of how he dressed or what he thought were no longer of importance to him, he would choose the first evening on which he'd worn his blue and gold-piped Messenger's tunic. Not that he'd been invulnerable to Margaret's laughter as he'd cycled into the dusk. It had hung about him until – in the privacy of an empty schoolroom – he'd folded tunic, trousers and shirt on a desk top next to almost identical kit. The following morning – the forerunner of every morning that would follow – Harry Plimsoll, the gangling schoolboy lover of a grocer's delivery lad, knew that such barbs of sarcasm would never dent his confidence again.

–You'll hardly thrive on a teacher's salary, my laddie. Look at the Tomlins. He's forty if he's a day and they're still as poor as a brace of missionaries. And, anyway, what do you suppose you could teach anyone?

–English, I suppose, Mother.

–Indeed? And just where's the money to come from to put you through Teachers' College? Does it occur to you that your father and I have been supporting you for the best part of seventeen years? Quite time you started bringing something into the house, if you want my opinion. I'd been apprenticed three years when I was your age. Has it crossed your mind we might be entitled to expect something back after all we've done for you?

*

Not until three months later does an answer to his mother's question present itself. The dusk of New Year's Eve is thickening around Harry when it occurs to him.

–Mother, I'm astounded. All these years I'd imagined I was your son. Now I discover I was no more than a bloody insurance policy.

The rejoinder floats from his mouth, smooth as a mine suspended from a parachute and just about as devastating in effect. Certainly not the kind of smart observation to be used, within hours, in the course of the unavoidable family row that would coincide with the end of 1944.

On the chilly landing, Harry folds his arms tightly and scratches his armpits. He waits for that moment when blood will tingle again through his fingertips. It is a ritual he has perfected in a house where he is never warm. For a moment he considers switching on a light. He decides against this on the grounds that his father may call up from the hall to discover why his son is sitting cross-legged in the gloom contemplating an old wooden sea chest.

Very softly, Harry imitates the steady jug jug jug of an approaching Heinkel. In this way he reassures himself that his singing voice has truly broken. This clinches any argument as to whether he should, or should not, continue to sing in the church choir. A regular six-months course of masturbation twice daily had yielded little result. And then, one blissful Sunday in mid-July, his solo during Matins had faltered in mid-phrase. To the embarrassment of organist and congregation – but not his own – his sweet treble had plunged with Icarian speed to the jagged rocks of a basso profundo. This diversion, recollected with delight, does little to dispel his apprehension about the impending maelstrom.

All very well to have cajoled his parents into agreeing – reluctantly – to his attending the local Teachers' College a mere fifteen minutes' bike ride away. To have made a nonsense of the interview deliberately, so ensuring the letter of rejection in his inside pocket, has to be accounted provocative and Harry knows it. The immediate prospect causes his guts to churn as they have done, throughout adolescence, each time the air-raid warning sirens wail.

He casts around frantically for possible allies at the supper table when it is revealed that, if he is ever to become a teacher, he will need to leave home. Would

Uncle Cliff help? Unlikely. Godfather he might be but his interest in Harry has been minimal. Aunt Winifred? Harry is certain she'll opt out on the grounds of being a Plimsoll only by marriage. Vinnie is his one hope. He smiles, convinced that his grandmother alone might sense his growing need to break free. Would she – he faces the worst possible outcome – provide him with bed and board until the autumn, should he be told to pack by midnight?

–Harry?

John Plimsoll repeats his question querulously before his son is aware of it.

–What is it, Father?

–What are you doing, mucking about up there in the dark?

–Just tidying things in the chest on the landing. . .

–On New Year's Eve? Not joining the Navy tomorrow, are you?

–Might come in useful when I go to college. . .

–Nonsense. You'll only be along the road. Day students don't need luggage. You might come down and give your mother a hand. . .

–She hasn't asked me.

–Why do you have to wait to be asked? You might at least lay the table; put all this artistic talent of yours to some use. . .

–Give me five minutes.

Harry levers himself up and does an almost perfect handstand on the lid of the sea chest. Just for a moment, he considers pre-empting all the wrangling, tears and unremitting silences by volunteering for the Army. The fatuousness of doing so, with the end of the war in view, occurs to him instantly. The Allies are poised to land in Europe and he is no hero. He has not the slightest intention of being killed, as was his own hero, great and beautiful Wilfred Owen, while the Armistice details are being typed.

He climbs the second staircase. In the sub-arctic comfort of the bathroom he scrubs his face and hands.

★

15

–Winifred, don't fuss. I shall not catch cold. And if you had a glass of my elderberry now and again instead of that gnat's water you're pleased to call lemonade it might do something to thicken your blood, my girl.

Vinnie pulls herself to her feet. She stands erect enough except for a slight hunching of her shoulders that both Winifred and Margaret Plimsoll have observed in their own husbands. Ignoring the possibility that a stray white hair might drift into her portion of tinned pears set in raspberry jelly, Vinnie pats her curls lightly and tugs a cardigan from the back of her chair. With a swift – almost feline – glance she confirms that Margaret is watching her with a suffering and limpid stare. She also notes John has half risen from his chair. Vinnie sniffs and moves towards the kitchen door.

Steadying herself with the doorknob, she turns and sets her porcelain teeth with what she trusts is a perceptible crunch. For all she cares, the assembled family can take this as a determined jutting of her chin. Her sole concern is to check those phrases that rise in her throat from transforming disaster to chaos. A desire – for instance – to assure Margaret that she has no intention of sticking an overpowered old grannie's nose into something that does not directly concern her. Vinnie savours the chance of informing Margaret that vicious asides about one's mother-in-law should not be uttered carelessly in a public air-raid shelter lest they be retailed. Careless talk can indeed prove costly, she reflects, as she smooths a hand on her cherry-red party frock, quite forgetting she has been eating pickled onions and is not wearing her old gardening overall.

About her reproof to Winifred she cares less than nothing. Winifred is less involved than any of the family in the immediate crisis. Vinnie notes that her younger daughter-in-law is silently fiddling with a new sapphire ring. The old woman sniffs a second time, sure that her remark to Winifred hit home. Vinnie has suspected, for more than a month or so, that Winifred's lemonade is spliced with gin from a flask in one of her many handbags.

16

Before stepping down into the kitchen she looks John in the eye. Beneath his obstinacy and an increasing terror of showing warmth to anyone, he is still and always will be the auburn-haired young artificer dashing home from the dockyard blithe and penniless to borrow enough to join his pals at the yacht club.

Without dropping her glance, she lunges straight for the heart.

–I shall go and talk to him. He's the only grandson I have. Since Dunkirk.

★

It can only be his grandmother. Harry associates the steady and slocking steps with Vinnie, as he has done since childhood. There have been moments when he has intended to ask why her shoes are always half a size too large for her feet. But not this moment. Not as she waits one pace behind him on the frosty concrete. He blows his nose and continues to stare through the skeletal lilacs and the gaunt syringa. Being apprehensive that any kindness she might voice could prompt a further outburst of weeping, he does not turn towards Vinnie. Should she or anyone else have asked what – of all that had occurred during the past half hour – had most upset him, Harry would without hesitation have replied his bad luck in having two parents who yet again appeared intent on his public humiliation. And, should this claim be countered by a demand for earlier instances of such humiliation? Harry – unable to reduce the stars to any known configuration through his tears – would happily catalogue examples. First he might cite the insistence that he remain in grey flannel shorts until his sixteenth birthday on the threadbare pretext that only labourers' children were put into longs earlier than that.

Since his grandmother still says nothing, Harry has time to think of another instance. He calls to mind his embarrassment at having to leave birthday parties – until just before Christmas – at no later than half past nine. Who among the other sixteen and seventeen-year-old party-goers ever really believed there was always an extra shift as a Civil Defence Messenger to be filled?

–Well, Captain Oates? Do you intend to freeze to death out here in a fit of self-pity?

–You needn't think I'm going in there again to be laughed at.

–Don't be ridiculous, Harry. You're a Plimsoll and you don't run away. You bounce back like the rest of us. As for laughter . . . you could do with a darn sight more of it in this house. I mean a bit of simple laughter. Maybe a naughty chuckle now and again, too. 'Tennyrate, not those McCawdie sneers your dear mother goes in for.

–So you do think they're behaving in a cruel and stupid way?

–Your father's not a cruel man and don't ever let me hear you say he is. A lot of laughter's been knocked out of him. Never did have any business sense . . . dashing back to England in the middle of a slump and having to peddle vacuum cleaners . . . I ask you. . .

–So, why's he taking it out on me?

–He isn't. You don't know how to handle him and he can't stand up to that mother of yours. Her trouble is she never could cope with affection. Bullying's all she understands. Comes of a family of monsters, of course. What else would you expect from a Scot? All of 'em raised on porridge and sour chapels in a bitter climate. Well, there's no changing her and he would have her.

–Then at least you admit Mother's taking it out on me? Maybe she's jealous, in a way. Didn't you hear Father say she could have been a teacher, too, but her mother insisted she helped at home?

–What else would you expect of Old Mother McCawdie? Don't quote her to me. Called me a prostitute just because I used a drop of walnut juice to stop my hair going grey. Oh, yes. That all came back to me. . .

–You're joking?

–This is no evening for fibs, Harry. Tell you something else, too. They had to send a constable running after Mother McCawdie. As God's my judge, they did. With all hers airs and graces, she abandoned her children to waltz off after her second husband. Forgotten to tell him she'd four children already, hadn't she? Thought all that might perk you up a bit. Mind you, repeat anything I've said to any of them in there and you'll never go to college.

Vinnie has put only one foot wrong during this conversation. She has spoken directly and without in any way patronising her grandson. That – as they are beginning to say in forces canteens around the country – is fair enough. She has implied that Harry should not think with his tongue without considering first to whom he is speaking. That is prudent. And then – hoping that she could turn his thoughts outward to contemplate the future – she has touched on the possibility of his going to college.

This results in a further uncontrollable bout of weeping. Vinnie takes Harry in her arms and turns him so that he faces her. He continues to sob into her shoulder. He snivels that there's no point in returning to the subject; that he will be forced into some beige existence in a solicitor's office or a local bank. She waits with some impatience for him to stop. Her grandson's body is no great protection from the light drizzle that is beginning to dampen her cardigan.

–Harry, listen. It was you who used the word stupid about your parents. You know, it's you who's the only stupid one at this party. Once you can see that, I've no doubt we'll have you at college next autumn with the best of them.

Harry blows his nose with such force that Vinnie warns him of a possible nose bleed. He manages a brief laugh and becomes aware that they are both beginning to shiver.

–Yes, I know I'd be able to go to college if it were up to you. But it isn't. Anyway, why am I being so stupid?

–You'll get nothing for nothing in any market, my boy. First, look me in the eye and tell me what it is you're really after. No nonsense, eh? Is it a teacher's cap and gown? Do you want to starve in a garret scribbling verses? Or do you want out of this house at any price? The truth, Harry. None of your fancy words.

He breaks from Vinnie's embrace. He does not look her in the eye. Instead, he holds her with his right arm round her waist. She is his only ally and he has the wit to know it.

–I want to be myself and I just don't think I can be if I stay here. Well . . . only in odd corners. You see, Vinnie . . .

She stirs a little as he addresses her by her first name. Then she laughs. If it makes him feel more adult to think of her as Vinnie, she's no objection. For a moment it makes her feel twenty once more.

–I'd better say that again. I can be myself, Vinnie, when I come to stay with you. Not that I can at Winifred's and Cliff's. And I can be myself when I'm with one of my friends . . . one or two, actually. So, I guess I do want out. Tell you something in confidence. I messed up the interview at that college down the road deliberately. You see, if I could only get away, I could be myself all of the time. Just away from them all. Of course, after the war I want to travel. See for myself these places in Europe that people have been dying for.

–Doesn't seem too unreasonable to me. If I'd a brass farthing other than your grandfather's pension, I'd lend you the money. Looks like we've got a roamer in the family. Aren't you ever going to settle, Harry? No lady friend yet?

–Well, there is someone. Sort of. A bit early for all that if I'm going to travel, though.

–Harry Plimsoll. I'm not deaf, dumb, blind and silly and can't hold my water. You've the family nose, as Alice would have said. I know what that means in a man. If you can't be good – be careful.

–Really, Vinnie . . .

–Someone needs to tell you a thing or two, my lad. It won't be those parents of yours, I'll bet my knickers. Took 'em fifteen years to produce you. D'you know, your father once tried to tell me about some tribe abroad and I didn't

20

for the life of me know what he was blithering about. Mother – he said – the men are filthy beasts who have relations with their womenfolk when they're unwell. I'd peeled half the shallots before I'd fathomed out what he meant. Laughed so much I nearly sliced my thumb.

–So, what did he mean?

–That you can work out for yourself while you're on your way to another college interview. In the meantime, get in there and apologise. On second thoughts, wait in the kitchen. Make a decent cup of tea for us all. None of Winifred's maiden's water, d'you hear me?

–If you say so.

–I do, Harry. Then, with a bit of luck, you'll be wearing a red and black scarf in September.

–Apologise, though? For what?

–For nearly putting the kibosh on any chance of college you'll ever have. In.

Vinnie frees herself from her grandson's arm and shoves him towards the kitchen door. She watches as he dabs his face and then combs his hair. Just as she is about to tell him to straighten his shoulders, he turns.

–What was all that about red and black scarves?

–Just find that tea-pot, will you, and leave me to do my bit?

★

In the unlit kitchen, Harry turns off the gas a third time. He judges that things cannot be going too badly since no laughter filters under the closed dining room door. He does hear his father's voice raised in protest, once, at something that has been said. Vinnie's reply is equally firm though the words are indistinguishable. Some minutes later, Cliff's somewhat ponderous tones drift through like an unintelligible broadcast from a distant radio station. Hearing only the voice, Harry notes – for the first time – that a quarter of a century in a London suburb has not eroded Cliff's Hampshire burr. He also wonders what his uncle's contribution to the family council might be.

21

Ten more minutes pass and Harry becomes restless. He feels himself to be a participant in some grotesque party game. Soon he will have to open the door and face the crowd, quite ignorant of decisions taken or of what might be required of him. He perches on the high kitchen stool next to the gas stove and folds his arms. The next few days will not be pleasant. They can be no worse than he has come to expect whenever he has attempted to assert himself. For two days most certainly – three is the record yet to be broken – there will be a wounded silence. Breakfast will be on the table at precisely eight thirty if he cares to come down and eat it. Should he, however, prefer not to be the immediate object of his mother's mute reproach then bacon and eggs will congeal on the top of the gas stove. Should he attempt to placate her by joining her at the table, she will prop *The Daily Telegraph and Morning Post* against her latest tea cosy and scan it as though Harry has no past existence pertinent to her and no plan which could be of even marginal interest.

No one could pretend Margaret Plimsoll is uncivil. Harry can predict the exact shape of her sapless olive branch.

–There'll be lunch at one o'clock if you deign to be here. Just let me know your comings and goings. That's all. Good food can't be wasted.

He recalls earlier and naif efforts to work on what he mistook for a truce by offering to wash up after breakfast or to queue for the new issue of ration books. The olive branch was snapped with a sigh.

–Don't put yourself out on my account. I've certainly no intention of doing so on yours after what you said yesterday.

Et bloody cetera. So Harry concludes his vignette of the immediate future with his phrase of the moment. On more careful consideration he is forced to accept that any thaw will be more protracted this time. Not that he has any intention of going for unconditional surrender. That would entail a public recantation – within the next five or ten minutes – of any wish to leave home until his call-up papers arrive. He itemises the concessions that may be exacted. Should they include the usual sanction on washing dirty shirts, he wonders whether it would be feasible to arrange something with Vinnie. In return for the scrubbing of soiled neckbands there could be an offer to clean her cottage during college holidays.

He becomes conscious of pain in his right index finger. He sucks it and then binds his handkerchief around the nail on the off-chance that there may be blood. Finally, he spits the loose shred of flesh at which he has been nibbling into the sink.

There's still no rattling of the door-handle that will call his to the conference table. He remains in the darkness firming up his plan of action. The only offer he will make will be an unqualified apology for a rash tirade against his mother's family. Not that he privately retracts one word.

–*The very idea. Saucing your father like that in front of his own family. If he says you're not going anywhere, that's exactly what he means. You should have had one of my brothers for a father. You'd soon have had your ears boxed, big as you think you are. . .*

–*Mother, I have my own father and I'm damned glad of it. . .*

–*Watch your language in this house. . .*

–*Sorry, Father. As for your brothers, Mother . . . one's a retired sergeant-major bossing poor lunatics around and the other's driven all his children from home except the runt of the litter. And where's that poor creature? In a hospital for nervous diseases. I just thank my stars I wasn't born in either of their prison houses. . .*

–*How dare you? Either one of them would have thrown you out on the streets for what you've just said. . .*

–*Not a chance, Mother. I'd have been off like an escaped prisoner of war. . .*

–*The boy's mad. John . . . assert yourself. Am I to be spoken to like this in my own house?*

White with fury, John Plimsoll stands nonplussed at the far side of the table to confront his gangling son. There is no parallel instance from his own boyhood on which he can draw. The scarlet-faced teenager who sits gnawing his lips is a stranger. Any of John's unvoiced expectations that Harry will progress uneventfully from school to some interesting office work

23

*and then – within a few years – to a wife and a couple of nippers,
are spattering like homesteads in the aftermath of a raid.*

*Once again – as he has done for months – John concludes that his
son is becoming more remote and inaccessible as the days pass.*

*–You will apologise to your mother and leave the table. College
is OUT. Do I make myself plain?*

Harry relights the gas. Having blown out the match, he
wonders how differently his father might have handled
the whole college project had he not returned exhausted
from a Docklands factory each evening. He thinks also of
his grandmother's advice in the garden. Applying it to his
father he has to concede he knows less of the man than
of Harding or of Joe. Any attempts at discussion collapse
into monosyllables of prejudice and commonplaces.

Invitations to play tennis at the weekend are declined
and the only outings offered in return are to heavy
engineering exhibitions. Even attempts to use music as a
bridge between father and son have been fraught. To be
told one plays the piano like a colt with a crowbar is no
encouragement.

The kettle begins to spit and protest. Harry guesses it
needs refilling. As tap water and hot metal fight, he
considers his father's seeming passion for gardening. It
could be a patriotic urge to produce fresh vegetables. It
could be an inheritance from country forebears. It could,
however – bearing Vinnie's words in mind – be an escape
from his wife's tongue. Yet, if so . . . what had filled in the
hours when there had been no overtime before the war?

An image from Harry's childhood presents itself. John
Plimsoll in his work shed under a naked lamp instructing
tall slim apprentices in the use of lathe and soldering
irons. The outline of those apprentices ten years back
seems not too dissimilar from Joe glimpsed in a doorway.
Or himself. And yet there appears to be nothing John
Plimsoll – Works Manager and expert – wishes to teach
his own son. Harry wonders at which exact moment his
father dismissed him as impractical, other than as an
eight-year-old designer of model theatres. If not then,
well, perhaps later. Possibly when discovering a teenage

24

son poring over an encyclopaedia while a puncture in his cycle remained unrepaired.

–When are we going to get this cup of tea, Harry? Thought you'd zoomed off in a Spitfire to pick the leaves in Assam.

Vinnie Plimsoll leans against the kitchen door-frame. Her back is to the light. Neither she nor her grandson care very much whether the nod of her head or an elaborate waving of her index finger against her lips is seen or guessed at by their relatives. Behind her the family makes frenzied small talk about a possible date for the landing in Europe. Winifred is adamant that it really is Eisenhower she sees speeding through the High Street in a jeep on his way to Bushey Park. Margaret is more cautious and suggests it could be an actor who is his double. She reminds them all that Monty has one. Why not Ike?

★

–Very well, Harry. I accept your apology. Naturally I shall do my best to forgive all the cruel remarks you've made about my family. But of course you can't expect me to forget.

Harry hears his mother's words flooding across the table. They circumvent the Dundee cake and swill around those few sticks of celery that remain in the cut-glass vase. Having heard them so often he hears but does not listen. They are as predictable as a statement of Pythagoras' Theorem or the proposition that in Mediterranean climates one should expect hot dry summers and warm wet winters. Vinnie dices a segment of Stilton cheese and does not raise her eyes. No one ranged around her can guess how often she too might have heard the words before. Privately she compares Margaret's litany of woe to an unforeseen storm from which one should shelter until it passes and the more pleasurable pursuit of tending a garden can be resumed.

It is Winifred who speaks after some coughing and passing of cigarettes. Harry is cheered by his aunt's intervention. To him, Winifred is a zonking bore and a laughable snob. Yet he also recollects his mother's dismissive snort about her sister-in-law. Winifred the Peace-Maker. As she glances brightly round the dining table, Harry has the sense of hearing an unsteady all-clear after a heavy night raid. Winifred does not care for inaction. Since Edmund's death she has taken to poodles and bazaars and neighbours' wartime problems with the zeal of a school captain looking for a commission.

–So now . . . what's to be done?

By elimination, Harry deduces it is his father who will speak. This reasoning is faulty for he has overlooked one marginal factor. Has Cliff Plimsoll been brooding again on the death of Edmund and drunk more elderberry wine than anyone noticed? None of the family could assert or deny this. It does occur to both Harry and Vinnie, as Cliff clears his throat, that perhaps he foresees some distant New Year's Eve when their common surname will be known only through the existence of Harry.

–It's not for Winnie, or me, to get involved in all this. Even so, you are my godson, Harry. If all this college business turns out to be anything more than pie in the sky, I shall let you have a fiver at the beginning of each term. One other thing. With all this clothes rationing nonsense I'd like you to have Edmund's black coat and striped trousers. The kit he wore when your aunt's brother was decorated at the Palace. . .

Vinnie's mouth works furiously in the silence. Both her sons – noting this – hope she will not weep at the mention of Edmund. Margaret contemplates Harry and he does not fail to catch the amused triumph at the back of her eyes. It is the offer of inherited clothes. She is remembering earlier rows when she has pleaded poverty so that Harry has had to wear turned and cut-down suits while, from somewhere, she has just scraped the money for a fur coat.

But Harry smiles. Neither Margaret Plimsoll nor anyone in the room can know of the warm blue afternoons five summers past when he'd perched on Edmund's crossbar

26

deep into the Surrey commons in search of early black-berries.

–Thanks very much, Uncle Cliff. And Aunt Winifred. I'd be chuffed – that is, I'd be delighted – to have Edmund's suit. But . . . well . . . when am I supposed to wear it?

Harry realises he is forcing the issue. He knows he's lowered the prow of his landing craft as surely as many more will be lowered, within months, at points along the northern coast of France. John Plimsoll lights another cigarette. Is taking a sip of tea. Will Harry suffer another raking on the foreshore with thirty rounds rapid? Vinnie's slight flutter of an eyelid – no more than any observer would attribute to a nervous twitch – could indicate that an invitation to discuss terms might be imminent.

–You've your grandmother to thank for what might be a workable solution. Now don't go running away with the idea that you're about to gallivant off to some hotbed of reds and layabouts . . . and worse. If you can get yourself into the Teachers' College at Winchester, then we'll see what can be done.

–That's terrific, Father. But why Winchester?

–There you go again. Why this? Why that? Questioning everything. I'll tell you why. Because I damn well say so. It amazes me you don't know why. Seem to have everything else off pat. Your grandfather was Postmaster there. That's why. Your grandmother here still has friends in the city. That's why. So, if you've got any idea of larking about in some students' hostel you can forget the whole business.

–But of course I'll stay with any of Grandmother's friends.

There is evidence of relaxation around the table. Margaret suggests that as an act of contrition Harry should make some more tea. He agrees readily. As he carries dirty cups through to the kitchen, Winifred wonders whether Vinnie's one-time lodger might still be alive. John hopes not, for it would be one German less. Vinnie admits she's had it on her conscience always that she might have been giving food to someone who was possibly a Nazi even in 1937.

27

Swooping like a Spitfire pilot by the kitchen sink, Harry catches one of the best teacups, so averting a fresh catastrophe. He has been concentrating frantically on some public statement that will not only demonstrate he's a dutiful son but will also serve to hold his father to his promise long after the family has dispersed.

–Tea's nearly ready. I do hope you're all going to come down to Winchester to see me. I shall be able to offer you tea. Father, I've just thought of something. . .

–What now?

–Will I need a permit for Winchester? Isn't it in the restricted area now they're preparing for the second front?

*

16th February 1944

Just picture for yourself, Veronica, the dining-room window pushed up and *warm* sunlight streaming in as I write you these few pages. A hint of spring already and we're still only half-way through February. With rumours of an Allied landing growing by the week, life in wartime London is nearly worth living. John's working full out at the factory and, with Harry not due until whenever he cares to breeze in, I have the place to myself. So there's really no excuse for not sitting down to thank you for the truly unexpected parcel which arrived (a bit battered) yesterday.

Real tea again! My dear – if you only knew the times I've sat here these past years, with a potful of floor sweepings, thinking back to those days in the Yacht Club where tea still had the smell of plantations in the Ngong Hills. Well – I'm raising my cup now and saying Here's To You Both. Too frightening to realise it's more than seventeen years since you waved us off at Mombasa. If you could see me now, Ronnie – a middle-aged housewife counting herself lucky to be able to afford a daily. And a gardener twice a week who's so blind he stamps to death on Friday half he's planted on Tuesday. As for the food we have to put up with! I'm sick of knocking up sausage toad that doesn't contain enough red meat to make a vegetarian blush. I'm sure the general public gets only what's left over after the West End Clubs and hotels have taken their pick. Not that my menfolk would mind. John would eat poison so long as he didn't have to cook it. Harry – who'll be seventeen this year – does nothing but eat. There are times when I think it would be easier running a canteen.

Next time you go to a do at the Provincial Commissioner's residence tell him, from me, the England you all remember is changing. If my son's anything to go by it's not for the better. Thank your lucky stars Ronnie that your bairns were brought up in Africa. There'll be no stability here in England after this war's over. My brother-in-law (Winifred's husband) is on the Borough Council. From what he's heard we shall most certainly have socialists in at Westminster. We all know what that will lead to – Jack's as good as his master, as your better half would say.

Harry comes home from stints as a Civil Defence Messenger with so many wild ideas he sounds like Harry Pollitt or old Maxton.

Neither I nor his father can say or do a thing right these days. I'm past caring about getting my head snapped off. Now I know you'll think I'm giving you the old palaver, so just what do you think of this for an example?

A couple of weeks back I bought myself a new top coat. After all, John is Works Manager now so I can hardly go round looking like a cleaner. Anyway, I spotted this model in Kensington (not in that cheapjack place Pontings – we're not reduced to that yet) so I popped in to try it on. My dear, when the Jew-boy who manages the department told me the price I nearly collapsed on the floor. He kept muttering to me that I should feel how deep the pockets were. Eventually, I did. Lo and behold, there were sufficient clothing coupons inside to buy the coat. How could I refuse?

Having lugged it home and tried it on that evening, John asked what colour I'd say it was. Without a second thought I said Nigger Brown. Immediately Harry's on his feet telling me that nigger is an unpleasant word and that something like coffee bean would do just as well. Can you credit it? That's the thanks you get these days for keeping them on at school.

Our Harry becomes odder by the hour. I've little doubt my own mother would have dismissed him as a changeling. He certainly doesn't favour my side of the family. When he's not off to see friends he seems too ashamed to bring home, he's up in his room playing gramophone records. Either we have to suffer tuneless dirges by some Finnish genius we've never heard of or else it's all honky tonk by a yankee named Muller or Miller. If his father dares to suggest he turns the racket down because it's giving me one of my heads, we have another shouting set-out. All because John refers to it as coon music. What else should anyone call it? But oh, no. Another lecture from our son and heir on what a different world it's going to be when the Nazis are beaten.

You know, there are times when I just wish Harry would go off and get some girl into trouble. If that sounds a terrible thing to say, I simply mean it would serve to bring him down to terra firma and knock all this highfaluting nonsense out of him. If only my John had shown more business sense we'd have stayed out there with all of you, away from this. To suggest it was *I* who insisted on coming home just isn't true, as I'm sure you know. Things might have been very different had we stayed on. Instead of lolling about dreaming over a book, Harry would have had his work cut out as a Cadet District Officer. More sport and exercise would do a darn sight more for him than reconstructing the world on the lines of schoolboy discussion groups.

Of course, I feel I can tell you all this. There's no one here I can unburden myself to. John's either exhausted and doesn't want to be bothered after supper or else he gets ratty and tells me I've got time to think of constructive suggestions. How can I know what's best? I feel I know more of Joe, the ginger-haired boy who delivers our groceries, than I do of my own son. As for talking about it to old Vinnie – she's as crafty as ever and will take Harry's part just to spite me. Don't even suggest Winifred. She's still the fool you found her to be when you were last over on long leave.

Enough of my woes. I've just topped up my cuppa and the most wonderful idea has struck me. In a couple of years an insurance policy we've been paying on Harry comes up. Matures is the word, I think. (Mature? Harry!) Anyway he's not likely to be at home when that happens. At twenty-one he'll no longer be our responsibility. Can you begin to guess what's coming? There should be ample for me to sail out and see you. Naturally John would come with me, if he can be spared from whatever the factory does after the war. How about that then for my own post-war planning? I can see it all . . . picnics on the slopes of Kilimanjaro again with fresh avocado sandwiches . . . pawpaw for breakfast after watching one of the piccanins shin up to pick it. To hear the *smiling* and *polite* waiters in the Ocean Bar welcoming one with Jambo Donna Margaret . . . Habare? I almost weep to think of it after all these grey and dreadful years.

And now I must finish. We too have our tiny excitements. This evening John and I are off to the Theatre on the Green. One of Winifred's endless Charity do's. There she'll be in the foyer, glittering like a Christmas tree with too much unsuitable jewellery. The Attlees are coming. She tried for Winston (trust her) but she's having to make do with the understudy. Talking of the great, I read your news about Berrington-Clough with a sad shake of the head. There was always something downright odd about that couple wasn't there? So she didn't even wear black for the funeral? I'm not surprised. Just what was this mysterious bug he picked up on one of his Congo trips? Not what priceless Winifred would call Vernal Disease was it? We always did have our doubts about that whole rugger team of houseboys they felt the need to employ. (Or do I mean *he* felt!?)

There's really nothing I can send except my love and the promise that *We'll Meet Again Some Sunny Day* as the Horses' Sweetheart sings. But then you've been spared her out there. Just play *Tea for Two* and think of us sometimes as you sip a gin and fresh lemon in the Club.

Love to you both,
Maggie.

P.S. Harry intends to be a teacher. Off to train in Winchester so that he can impose some of his cranky ideas on the unsuspecting. He'll end up like those poverty-stricken mission teachers degrading themselves by sharing Indian corn with the local tribesmen. Do I know this new hymn you mention: *Sikelele Afrika*?
I don't know where it will all end but I do know that I must . . . and pronto. Two o'clock and my rice pudding is ready in the oven. Coloured with cocoa this week to give it a bit of a zip!

★

A mile to the north of the Thames there is a collection of what Jeremy Bentham tells his sixth-formers are potential long barrows. This allusion – accompanied by a shake of the head – seems strikingly apt to Harry and he recalls it each time he passes the spot. There are ten of these shelters clustered around the school. Between them – but not for another three or four years – there will be avenues of turf and shrubs. On this particular day in mid-February 1944 any stray blades of grass could be counted on one hand. The heavy soil between the shelters is very evidently tended. Potatoes and spring vegetables have been planted by pre-pubescent hands eager to help – even indirectly – the cause for which their uncles, fathers and cousins are fighting. That their contemporaries in rural Germany may be similarly employed does not occur to these schoolboys. Should it do so, the idea would be dismissed as of no relevance.

Although the land is cultivated at ground level, the protruding shelters and the soil which covers them are – after more than four years – swathed in couch grass. This gives them the appearance of long barrows. On that which lies farthest from the school and nearest a lane that runs between Hampton and the new arterial road, there is one figure sprawled on his stomach. Harry Plimsoll: sixth-former (but also pupil teacher), boyfriend of Noreen Humby (but friend and also lover of Joe Gibbs), and rebellious son of Margaret & John Plimsoll. Harry's blazer is folded beside him and on it rests an elongated drum of colouring crayons. Brows furrowed against the unexpected sun and tongue-tip extruding between his teeth, he pins a sheet of cartridge paper to a drawing board.

As he edges a blue crayon from right to left he is conscious of falsifying the Thames in some ways. His line is as authentically blue as any that may be found in an atlas, yet the river he knows is pewter or sludge green or often grey dappled with gilt depending on the altering light. He adds some smaller squiggles. Even accepting them as conventional symbols of the Wey, the Colne and the Brent, he is irked that they will never convey the swelling river that contains so many fish, likewise swimmers, not to mention offal and occasional suicides.

He discards the blue crayon. Before picking up the scarlet, he finishes a russet apple and tosses the core into the open doorway of an adjacent shelter. His eyes linger a moment on the shadow. It does not seem likely that the shelters will become mass graves. He hears his father's voice retailing tragedies that never make the headlines. Direct hits on Whitechapel and New Cross. All civilians. No uniforms – except the firemen and the ambulance drivers. No one armed or with at least the fighting chance of Wilfred Owen.

Harry wishes he could use the scarlet crayon to begin a poem rather than having to circle in the ancient bridge towns and former villages. Leaving Kingston unmarked, so that the first-formers might guess at it, he wonders how far he should stray from orthodox geography. Would the history of Staines or the literary associations of Twickenham be frowned on by Dr Garstone – should he choose to saunter in? Harry chews the butt end of the scarlet crayon impatiently. Once again he knows he will have to temper adventurousness with prudence and it angers him. The Old Man will squeeze himself into a spare desk at the back of the room. This at least will guarantee that Harry's lesson is not punctuated by paper darts and carefully timed farts. Nevertheless the sallow and aquiline features of Dr Garstone have been known to intimidate nervous young teachers. To an unqualified sixth-former, the long brooding look and occasional brief note is close on unnerving. But it has to be borne. This is Harry's conclusion. On the Head's word the School Governors will judge – given that a place at Winchester is offered – whether Harry McCawdie Plimsoll is a fit and proper recipient of money from the coffers. An award for suitable books.

The hopeful recipient giggles and spits a shred of painted wood. Short of requiring him to forward a detailed receipt, it will be difficult for his Aunt Winifred's cronies who make up the governing body to check on how any award is spent. Harry contemplates not cloth-bound collected works but a succession of reserved seats for two in the gallery of the Whitehall Theatre. What would the Rural Dean make of a potential teacher who chose to fritter the evenings of each vacation thus? . . . Dear Rural Dean. Nice to see you. Joe and I have been watching Miss Phyllis Dixie's artistic chorus who pose motionless to show the crowds all they have. Their fannies, of course, are modestly concealed with more ostrich feathers than there were on Aunt Winifred's head when she was photographed being presented at court. Oh . . . later we popped in for a meal at the Lyons help-yourself and then we caught a fast train home. Sorry you didn't travel in our compartment but then we'd removed the small blue bulb. Just as well the trains are so slow. Joe and I managed to do it twice.

34

Dr Garstone passes within a few yards on his sit-up-and-beg bicycle. Harry very much hopes the Head has not heard laughter from the top of a shelter. A reason for it could easily be fabricated but laughing in solitude might not look well on a testimonial. He returns to his map after rolling up his shirt sleeves from his elbows. Not that he has any firm hope of enough strength in the sun to brown his limbs. He thinks enviously, for a moment, of the ease with which Joe's forearms seem perpetually bronzed and then – not without effort – concentrates his energy on a new approach to subject teaching.

With ludicrously slim experience, it already appears to Harry that the division of a day or week or even term into carefully ruled subject boxes can only be satisfactory in theory. He is sure that, in practice, all the seemingly different subjects must heave and shove against constriction by the neat and self-same lines of any timetable. Although even he guesses he hasn't quite the background to attempt any experiments during the afternoon, he feels it is a matter which might be followed up in a quiet chat with Hopalong Bentham. There is more breadth to the man than any of the walking wounded who do their best to cope. Harry cannot call to mind anyone other than Jeremy Bentham who could drift from the ablative absolute to local architecture and government and back into Latin with equal ease.

The green crayon begins to mark in the course of the Southern Railway's tracks across the middle Thames Valley. The map that is emerging is sufficiently colourful to corral the attention of twenty-eight eleven-year-olds. It might, with luck, preclude the tittering wretches from egging on the boldest to ask if their prefect-turned-teacher has a girlfriend. The prospect does not embarrass Harry. He has learned to parry veiled hints as to what he and Noreen might – or might not – be doing in the back row of the Luxor or the Regal. As he feathers in light cross strokes on the green line upriver from Staines, Harry considers the effect on such a class of revealing to them that at precisely the point where the railway meets the edge of the cartridge paper, he first wrestled playfully with Joe in a tussle they both knew would become gentler within minutes.

The crayons once more in their cardboard drum and the cartridge paper pushed from him, Harry drops his head on his folded arms and closes his eyes against the light. With the clean scent of the couch grass against his nostrils, he is not displeased to catch himself continuing to think about Joe. It puzzles him a little that he should not think equally about Noreen but this he attributes to the less fulfilling evenings he has shared with her.

It is not – Harry insists to himself – because Noreen would never allow him to do it before marriage whereas, with Joe, virginity didn't come into it. Having allowed himself to consider the topic consciously – and in daylight – he sheers away and tries to itemise where it is Noreen falls short in capturing his thoughts. Tennis is fine with Noreen. Joe has no interest in the game. Dancing close to Noreen is sexy but frustrating. Dancing with Joe doesn't arise but lying close to him is the tops. Chatting with Noreen about the future broadens the horizon to college (and for her to the West Middlesex Hospital) but not much beyond. Harry searches for some word, rather than a phrase, that will encapsulate just what it is that Noreen lacks. Spirit he discards with the supposition that she has a surfeit of that. Nor will enthusiasm to try something new serve. Her determination at the ice rink is evidence of that. His image of Noreen at the edge of the rink does not dissolve and he is sure he has the answer. Ice rink and dance halls and the river itself are no more than walking distance or a couple of coins on a bus. Yet, to Noreen, they are sufficient – just as her decision to train as a nurse does not encompass any adventurous journey to Barts or Guys. The West Middlesex – twenty minutes on the trolleybus – is her unquestioning choice.

Noreen's reaction to any of Harry's colourful hopes and plans can only be construed as mildly supportive. To the hazy outlining of a life away from the Thames Valley with no regular income until poems are sought by the posher weeklies she responds with a smile. Harry does not bracket this with his parents' tolerant disbelief. He regretfully has to accept that Noreen withdraws to an unenthusiastic distance whenever – with more passion than accuracy – he argues that, had Wilfred Owen lived, there would have been no assurance of roast beef for him once the Sam Browne had been handed in. With increasing glumness, he wonders if Noreen thinks secretly that H.McC.Plimsoll (Dip.Ed.) will soon have all his fire dampened by the endless drudgery of a weekly timetable. To counter that he decides on some fast talking between the fox-trot and the hokey cokey at the next Town Hall hop. Noreen must understand that there will be no dissipation of plans and energy in redecorating a flat or saving for a motor bike and side-car such as her father runs.

Without pausing to admit that Noreen might not wish to understand, Harry thinks further of their joint future and how Joe might or might not have some place in it. Would he perhaps become a vague and distorted memory if Noreen agreed to the use of her parents' house – even once a month – so that they could really do it properly? A real clothes off and under the eiderdown job. There are often moments when Harry would like to think so. Such a comparable experience would put him on the same footing as Paul Harding. At exactly this moment he is conscious of the need for another apple. Knowing he has none, his licks his lips and wishes he had a glass of cider. And the image of Joe – eyebrows raised and slight upward curl of a lip – rises before him.

The thoughts and resolutions that chase across Harry's mind become random and have far less order than his map. He blinks in the sunshine and mutters – Bugger being like Harding.

He sits up and swivels himself to sit cross-legged facing away from the school buildings.

–Joe's more than a bloody safety valve to preserve Noreen's virginity for a white frock.

He drums both fists in the couch grass and jumps to his feet.

–With Joe I'm me for the first time. No inhibitions. No restraints. No fucking pretence. His friendship assures me that I can be me.

Beyond munition workers returning from their morning shift, Harry sees a peaceful Europe through which he and Joe can travel first on pedal cycles and, later, on powerful motor bikes. They will see for themselves the wreckage that cruelty and greed and poverty have showered upon the young as a legacy. . .

–Plimsoll . . . Plimsoll . . . It's five past two. We're waiting in Garrick corridor and Mr Bentham's been asking where you are.

*

To gain admittance, one grips the greasy string lightly between thumb and forefinger and coaxes it through the letter-box until a key appears. John does this quite deftly. He is not a frequent visitor but he has the certain touch of a precision engineer.

Although this is the home of a relative, he is not sufficiently at ease to leave the door open behind him. He would like to. The windows are closed, too. He suspects they have not been cleaned for months. Even so, thin February sunlight filters like melting margarine through the grime and a protective frame of chicken wire. John notices this but is more concerned with the stench that assaults his nose. He analyses it as a mixture of patent medicines and dirty plates, topped up with unwashed dog blanket. The chenille-covered table by which he stands is littered with the detritus of at least three meals.

After waiting a full minute he calls through to the second room in an over-hearty way.

–Let's be having you then, Uncle Walter. John here. I've brought you a few bits and pieces.

A mongrel noses aside a threadbare blanket strung across the doorframe that leads to the bedroom. John snaps his fingers and it wanders towards him. A contorted wordless succession of noises comes from the further room. For one instant John fears his uncle might be choking. He then realises that dentures are being hooked into place. Another minute passes before Walter Cosser slides back the blanket and shuffles into the living room.

–Hello, my cocker. What blows you round this way then? Brought me Easter egg early, in case I don't see the winter out?

–You'll see plenty yet. I . . . well . . . I just dropped by to see how you're doing.

–That's kind of you, young Jack. Surprised you still knew the way.

–Now, now. We did send a card at Christmas.

–So you did. Kept it with the others to start the fire. Want a cup of tea? I was just about to make one.

Since the kettle has to be filled and the fire is down to an expiring ember John finds this difficult to believe. But he does lift a copy of *The Daily Herald* from a chair by the table and sit down.

–No need to trouble. I've had lunch in the canteen. Fact is, it's such a fine day I popped along to the market. Brought you a polyanthus for the window. There's a bone for the dog wrapped up there.

–You always were a thoughtful nipper. Nice colour, this flower. Knew red's me favourite, did you? Or is it a bit of yer mother's humour coming out in you?

–Didn't think you'd be keen on blue.

–Too right you are. If you're not going to have a drop of tea you can sit and watch me. The old hound's more frisky than me these days. Hold on now, Ramsay Mac. Hold on till I unwrap it.

While the kettle boils John watches his uncle's arthritic progress between fire and sink. The silk choker the old man wears has been slept in for more than a couple of nights. There are tattoos dating from before Victoria's Golden Jubilee on the grey forearms that lift the kettle. Walter sets the brown earthenware pot on a pile of magazines. He rinses two tin mugs but does not dry them.

39

–So, how's Vinnie? Going up in the world with the rest of you?

–She's in fine form. Had a nasty nose bleed at the end of last year but she's right as ninepence now. The rest of the family are pressing on, as they say. We're . . . we're all looking forward to a landing in Europe soon. That'll have Jerry on the run.

–There you go, Jack. There you go. Jerry on the run. That's all it is to you, ain't it? Getting Kaiser Bill on the run a second time round, eh?

–How else would you describe it, Uncle? This time they call themselves Nazis. . .

–And so they are, my cocker. And so they are. Fascists. The super race exterminating anyone who ain't all blond and brawn. . .

–All right. We don't need to go into all that again. Let's just make this a social call and forget the politics, even if Uncle Joe happens to be with us at the moment. . .

–'ere. Have this tea. If I had anything stronger you'd be welcome, even if you seem set fair to become a bloody capitalist. Stiff collar and tie and a bit of gents' natty suiting, I see. Now. How's that lad of yourn?

–He's coming up to seventeen soon.

–Is he just? Now he'll be ripe for helping to construct a new world. Things is going to be different, Jack, me old cocker. There'll be no going back to the means test and the soup kitchens. . .

John sips his tea. He recalls the uncle whose return from sea he would await in childhood. Presents. Outings. Brooding days in the kitchen towards the end of a leave when all had been spent up.

He pushes a Craven A across the chenille cloth. The dog farts but both men affect to notice nothing. As John looks up, Walter's faded but still penetrating glance is on him.

–All that's as may be. As for Harry . . . well . . . we don't talk politics or religion in the house, as well you know.

–I also know when you're dodging the issue, young John. Watched you growing up, didn't I? It don't surprise me how natural you play the grand Works Manager now.

40

Not at all. I well remember hearing you pretend you didn't know what yer old gran did to keep body and soul together. Oh, yes. I heard you lying to some wet-nosed doctor's brat. Didn't care to say old Sarah took in washing by the tubful, did yer?

—Now that's unfair, Walter. She'd always told us boys she did it as a favour.

—And at twelve it never occurred to you she 'ad her pride? Hadn't invented pensions then, had they? Took in washing as a favour. . . Marx-all-bloody-mighty. Ah well. Let it pass. But you're cocking a deaf 'un about your Harry, aren't you?

—There's nothing to tell. He's still in the sixth form.

—Is he now? Got a touch of me in him, has he? Dawned on him the family nest ain't the be all and end all?

John shifts uneasily and laughs just a little too heartily.

—Let's hope you're a better engineer than actor, John matie. Young Harry having growing pains, is he? You two want to watch it. Especially piss-proud Maggie. I might take it into my head one of these fine afternoons to meet the lad. I could tell him a few home truths down the boozer. Don't think I ain't got the fare put by. . .

—There's no call for that, Walter. You wanted to clear out and lead your own life . . . if this is what you want for your old age. We've respected that, so I'd take it as a favour if you left us alone.

—You patronising young bugger. Even talk like a boss in a Board Room you do, straight up. Ah well. Let it pass. What's young Harry going in for?

—He intends to be a teacher.

—That so? Well . . . there's teachers and teachers. One of them fancy places, is it? All Latin and Greek and fox the masses, is it?

—No. He'll work in what we used to call a Board School. English. . .

—That's good, Jack. That's good. He might come and help me string a few words together when he's trained. I quite fancy a bit of political work again when I'm over this lumbago. Got some really good jollop for it

41

this time, John. Whole bottle from this geezer down the market. Let me have it for next to nothing. . . Now . . . where was we? Harry. Yes. Which college is he down for?

John lifts his mug as casually as he can. He foresees Walter's ploy and needs a moment or so to frame an answer. Not that he supposes his uncle will use any occasional winnings from the dog tracks to appear at the college gates in Winchester. Far more likely the old man will stagger to the local reference library if given even half an address. And then? John's supposition is that within a few days there would be a list of book titles arriving for Harry. In Walter's usual bold neat capitals. Communist books.

–We're not certain yet. Now . . . anything I can do for you before I get back to the Works?

–Not away already, are you? It's barely two o'clock. Can't you please yourself? Bosses ain't frightened of the sack, are they?

–Have to set the men an example, Walter. We want the second front this year not next, you know.

–Have it your own way. Thanks for the ham and the Pale Ale. Make a nice tea for us won't it, Ramsay Mac? Likes his bowl of booze before his evening run, he does.

John leaves two pound notes on a chair by the door. More accurately he puts them on the cover of a dog-eared account of the great dock strike of 1889. Walter seems unaware of this gesture and stands in the doorway to watch his nephew begin his descent of the seven flights of stairs.

–How's Alice then?

–How should I know that, Walter?

–I was forgetting. She's a dead 'un to you all, too, now. Reckon you guessed Alice and me had our fun before you was thought of. I caught on years ago I was just useful to her. Got her aboard like. She was soon shinning up the companion way without her drawers. All officers and suppers after the opera it was for our Alice. Not saying

42

I wouldn't like to see her walk in, though. She liked a laugh. . .
–Look after yourself, Walter. . .
–Not likely anyone else will, is it? That boy of yours out with the girls yet?
–He's got his mind on other things. And so should you at your age. Cheerio.
The nails in John's leather shoes strike sparklers from the stone steps as he walks quickly down the echoing stairs of Peabody Buildings and into the Walworth Road. Walter listens to his nephew whistling tunelessly as Vinnie once did when uneasy.

★

At eleven thirty precisely Alice Dowsett goes out, closing the street door behind her. Her progress is observed by other residents of Wessex Avenue. Between blackout curtains or pre-war velours with ragged linings, they chart her course towards the junction with St Swithin's Drive. In some front parlours comments on her are offered to relatives or companions huddled by smouldering fires. In others, to mongrels or cats or parrots. There are one or two villas in which the words resound through empty rooms. This neighbourly interest in a newcomer never flags. The phrases in which it is expressed tell more, perhaps, of the speakers themselves than of Alice Dowsett.
–Here comes Lady Muck. Half past eleven as per usual. . .
–What a sight she do look. Got up fine enough for the Bishop's garden party. As if we don't know she's sailing off to the British Restaurant for a bowl of Brown Windsor and a helping of bangers and mash. . .
–How do she come by all them clothes these days? Ten to one it's that gentleman friend as brings her coupons of a Thursday. Brother? He's no blood relative of hers. You'd sit there believing me if I told you I was Gracie Fields.

43

–Eh, Gran? Gran? She's going past. 'er face is pink and white as your Sunday tea-pot. Reckon you could be right, gran. 'er's no better then she should be.

Alice will soon be seventy-six, on a day she was thrilled to share – when younger – with the unfortunate Russian Tsarina. She hears nothing of her neighbours' gossip as she strolls between bone bins lashed to lamp standards and pig bins overflowing with vegetable peelings. She guesses there may be comments but she does not care. Does she not own Lilac Villa (formerly Number 82) outright? Each time she approaches its aptly painted street door she recalls with gratitude the legacy of a County Alderman. Never with servility. She returns gratitude for gratitude. An account closed on both sides after a quarter of a century's pleasurable transactions.

Over her toast and home-made jam each morning, Alice smiles silently to herself in acknowledgement of the chances that have brought her to a comfortable harbour at last. In more analytical moments – when she has reread, say, a letter from a contemporary reduced to a bare pension – Alice admits that chance has been nudged a little by her willingness to bestow favours on more than several gentlemen. This is a phrase that occurs in the historical romances to which she is addicted. There is no question of subsistence on a pension at Lilac Villa. Has she not recently sold to a very gentlemanly little person on the far side of the city five Regency fob watches (four silver and the gold one reputedly a possession of Nelson's friend, Captain Hardy)? Who could dispute that the proceeds from these trifling mementos of the dear Major-General will ensure sherry each evening until Alice is eighty-six? And some nice coach tours through Scotland and Wales when the war is over.

As she turns into St Swithin's Drive to begin her descent, Miss Dowsett pauses. She is not breathless. The pause is part of her morning routine. Leaning on her walking umbrella she inhales with the vehemence of a singer. Exhaling, she smiles on Winchester. No more barrage balloons swimming up over the Dockyard from dawn to dawn. No more battling to put on her morning face before the smeared mirror in some labourer's scullery before returning to inspect the latest wounds and lacerations inflicted on dear Portsmouth. No further reason for Alice Dowsett to startle strangers in queues and shelters with the revelation that she is a displaced person. She has adopted Winchester. She concedes it may be a little longer before Winchester reciprocates. At the end of her very first week in Lilac Villa she was able to confirm the popular perception that country people are slower on the uptake. Her milkman had seemed a little confused when she informed him that she should not be considered as a stranger.

–I'm a Wintonian now, Mr Fairhall. I was a Pompite but now I've come to live among you, I'm a Wintonian.

Tip-tapping her way with a stateliness that rivals Queen Mary's, Alice descends to the dustier and more unfashionable shops.

Drawing level with Station Approach – though on the farther side of the road – she is very well aware of the train that is grunting at the down platform. The first of a trickle of passengers emerges into Station Yard. As he does so, Alice squares her shoulders and turns aside to absorb herself – so it might seem to passers-by – in the utility spring fashions that have been unenthusiastically displayed in a small window. It happens that the surround has been lined with mirrors to assist potential customers. Alice – though initially distracted by the no-nonsense box-pleats of a mauve two-piece – is neatly placed to study the approaching passengers.

She eliminates the women in bandeaus and the land girls in jodhpurs. In observing the men she uses her recollections of not one but two generations. As she scrutinises the khaki and the pale and dark blue uniforms she catches herself humming *Goodbye Dolly Gray* and stops in mid-phrase. Less because it dates from an earlier war than that this particular April morning is not to be associated with farewells. Only two youths advance towards her via the mirrors. The one with buck teeth and mudded cords she supposes might be making for a farm or to have come from working on a demolition site. Should he by an outside chance be stumping towards Lilac Villa, Alice decides that he will wait for a very long time before making for wherever the Teachers' College may be.

She is not repelled by her first glimpse of Harry. He appears to be unusually wholesome for a Londoner. Not at all pasty-faced or liverish. There have been few hours of sunlight over southern England since the previous autumn so Alice concludes a slightly bronzed face may be the residue of an adolescence concentrated on outdoor activities. She has no doubt as to the identity of the youth in a herring-bone hacking jacket and grey worsteds. His long neck comes from his mother's side. An anecdote resurfaces but only in part. Something about a naval gentleman four generations back bringing home a girl from Cádiz to the Scottish Highlands. She is fairly certain this does relate to Margaret Plimsoll's family and not to Flora Macdonald and Bonnie Prince Charlie. It would account for the darkness of Harry's skin and his high colouring. Alice continues to observe him as he waits to cross the road a little to her left. He turns once to glance at the tailboard of the last in a convoy of army trucks and she catches him in profile. For an instant Alice is no longer in Winchester. The hall is bright with laughter at dear Vinnie's Silver Wedding. Not Harry but eighteen-year-old John Plimsoll is moving towards her.

And then it is 1944 again. But the nose is the same. Young Harry has the family nose. Memorable and – as Alice and Vinnie agreed so long ago on the Common at Southsea – a very dependable guide to passionate gentlemen, some of whom have to be restrained with more than argument.

Alice is careful not to make the slightest movement with her umbrella though she distinctly feels a spot of rain. She is sure Harry has in no way become aware of her presence before he turns left into Wessex Avenue. Having counted sixty, she straightens a stray violet in her straw hat and continues down the hill trusting the rain spots will not develop into a shower. She concedes it to be a little early in the season for straw but Mr Stuart Hibberd had hinted – no more, for security reasons – at the end of the morning news that there could be a light touch of sunshine over southern England by noon. One could begin to trust the wireless again now that any possibility of invasion had passed.

That she should have a bit of luck at the library doesn't astound Alice. Yet again Lyndoe, her favourite Sunday astrologer, has proved dependable. She makes a mental note to write to him personally and ask for a signed photograph. It would look well on her writing bureau in the morning room next to the autographed studio portrait of Mr J.B. Priestley, whose fireside chats are so enjoyable, though Alice has read suggestions that he might have socialist leanings. Miss Fordingbridge places the novel that has been so long on order in front of Alice. They exchange conspiratorial smiles. These should not be mistaken for the smiles of anti-patriotic black marketeers. War – or so Alice often says with a laugh – develops a little guile in everyone. Miss Fordingbridge agrees – as she has on previous occasions. The bag of home-made fudge with which Alice has bribed her way to the top of the queue for *Bess of Hatfield* is almost empty. As Miss Fordingbridge date-stamps the *perceptive insight into intrigues surrounding the young Queen Elizabeth*, she confides there's expected to be a reshowing soon of *Fire over England* with Flora Robson as the Virgin Queen. Alice is ecstatic. She offers to buy seats for them both on Miss Fordingbridge's half day. The plump librarian flushes a little and stumblingly confesses that she has already promised to go with a friend in the Home Guard. Her hands are not visible from the far side of the counter as she speaks so that Alice cannot possibly see Miss Fordingbridge crossing her fingers. She has no wish to offend but she does fear public embarrassment. To have had Elizabeth's Tilbury speech rendered between the Reference Section and the Periodicals had been humiliating. To risk a repetition. . .

Alice thanks Miss Fordingbridge – a little frostily the librarian suspects – but she does promise a report on the novel. Encouraged perhaps by the volume in her string bag and perhaps by a light wash of sunshine on the pavements, Alice quickens her step towards the fish shop. Those passing nod to her or smile indulgently.

Trucks are converging by night and day on the restricted areas of the south coast. The landings in Europe are imminent and in bars they are taking bets on the exact date. Why shouldn't an elderly woman in an improbable chestnut wig sing *There'll Always Be An England*? And if her ripe contralto slithers to an impressive bass should anyone laugh? Nobody does as Alice hastens towards the fish shop on the corner of Cathedral Close.

*

Rhoda extracts her chewing gum and claps it to the underside of Gran Alverstoke's bamboo table. It is a habit she has recently acquired through observing G.I.s at a middle distance. Chewing gum – or so Rhoda convinces herself – binds her to the adult world of war more than she can ever hope to be while confined to Gran's front parlour. A pair of nylons would be preferable. They would convey, to all, the wearer's adult status as surely as a uniform. Until an unexpected movement in the stillness of Wessex Avenue distracts her, Rhoda concentrates her attention on a way in which she might wheedle nylons from Alfie.

Butter he manages – and sugar too – without complaint or difficulty. For birthdays and family gatherings he supplies a tin of over-sweet melon jam from under his battledress tunic. A ration store isn't usually overstocked with nylons. Rhoda perceives the difficulty and ruminates on the advisability of cultivating an American. Early evening it would need to be to avoid Alfie arriving unexpectedly in his little truck. She considers the advantages of joining the Cathedral Youth Club. It would sound respectable enough to Gran. The Club meeting hall – being near the

Market Cross – couldn't be better situated for chatting to G.I.s waiting to thumb lifts back to camp.

Rhoda's imagination warms. It would need to be a dark-haired bloke with smouldering glances. Some undiscovered he-man like Robert Taylor. Just as she begins to feel a glow at the back of her neck, while pondering how far this hero should be allowed to take advantage in return for a cascade of nylons, an unfamiliar sight interrupts her. A young man is knocking at Miss Dowsett's door.

–Gran. You'll never guess. Hey . . . Gran . . . wake up.

–Not them hooters again, is it? Them Nazis back?

–Course not. They won't never come back. Listen . . . you'll never guess.

–Sweets have come off the ration and you ain't chewing that gum no more. Don't you think, madam, as I can't guess what you gets up to the minute I rest me eyes.

–Well I'm not chewing now. Look in me gob and prove it. Now . . . if you don't want to know. . .

–Well go on, girl. What is it?

–She's got a visitor.

–How many times must I tell you to give people a name? Wouldn't have done when I was in service and that's a fact. Who's got a visitor?

–Miss Alice Violet Dowsett of Lilac Cottage, Wessex Avenue. That's who.

–'Tain't Thursday, is it? Not him she'd have us believe's her brother, is it?

–Wouldn't bother to wake you for that, would I? This one's no more than an overgrown schoolkid. Should I nip across and tell him she's out?

–There's others as can do that. Don't think I'm not up to your little tricks, my lady. Bad blood, like all yer father's lot. Lust's yer middle name. Hot for anything in a pair of slacks.

–What you on about, Gran? He's only a boy.

–Old enough to know his way around the gooseberry bush I'll be bound.

–Do give it a rest. I should go. I do help over there in the mornings, don't I?

49

–Be sharp about it then. That's all I'm saying. There's twelve o'clock striking. And no larking about with the neighbours watching. Don't go filling their mouths with gossip about this house. You just get back here smartish to put me spam and mash on. I'm not missing Workers' Playtime, visitor or no visitor. Mark my words, Rhoda . . . don't want no young tom cats sniffing round this doorstep.

With Gran's admonitions pounding her ears Rhoda closes the parlour door. She knows her progress to the street will be followed sound by sound. There cannot be too long a pause in front of the mirror in the passage. Having torn off her wrap-around overall, she cannot spare more than a moment to pat her ringlets and give them a shake. If only Gran would permit her a touch of powder and a dab of lipstick – natural shade, of course – there might be a chance to audition for Margaret Lockwood's understudy. This – or eloping with a G.I. – presents Rhoda with a desirable alternative to working in a smelly old canning factory. She vents her irritation with Gran by sticking out her tongue at the barbola work that surrounds the mirror. But not all her irritation. She deliberately slams the street door behind her. She is sure that Gran will not bother to leave her chair to check whether the noise stems from temper or a sudden gust of wind. The disruption of Wessex Avenue's midday tranquillity serves – as it happens – another purpose. Beyond the rubble and sprouting weeds where a land-mine fell, Harry hears it. He looks to his right as he sits on the steps of Miss Dowsett's double-fronted and follows Rhoda's scurrying steps. Once she has his attention, Rhoda waves. He is on his feet as she flits over the crazy paving and into the porch of what, she reminds herself, she should not refer to as Number 82.

–She's gone out.

–Well, I rather supposed she had.

–Gran said as I should slip across and let you know.

–Then you're a relative? I mean, she likes you to call her gran?

Rhoda laughs. It begins as a giggle. The kind of giggle she enjoys when Alfie drops his key down her back and then has to put his hand under her petticoat to fish it out. Gran has warned her about these giggles so she modulates the noise to a refined laugh. A lady-like trickle that wouldn't disgrace Anna Neagle or Greer Garson. She remembers to use her eyelashes and control her lips. Gran insists it's vulgar to show the gums.

–What a thing to say. I mean my own gran. Back there at 99. I come here most mornings to give a hand around the house.

–So, she's an invalid then? No one told me that.

–You do mix things up so. It's my gran's an invalid. This one here's gentry, see? What you come about, then?

Harry becomes wary. Mrs Blunt – being almost family through friendship with Vinnie – deserves some loyalty. Rather more than some since she will very possibly become his landlady and another potential ally. He does not doubt that, compared with London, this market town of Winchester is as gossipy as a village. It would be imprudent to chatter to a gawky teenager offering chewing gum from her cardigan pocket about someone to whom Vinnie had referred as a true friend.

–If you want to know . . . I shall probably be coming to live here for a couple of years, as a lodger.

Rhoda brightens a little. The visitor is no Robert Taylor and unlikely to be a direct source of nylons. He is – all the same – a cut above the farm boys. His teeth aren't beginning to stain already with tobacco and she is almost envious of his well-shaped lips. To Rhoda they are what Alfie would call very kissable. And the young man is not weedy. This last fragment of appraisal gives rise to an awful thought. Rhoda always voices immediately anything that occurs to her.

–How old are you, then?

–Me? Seventeen. As good as . . . why?

–How come you can be anyone's lodger? You should be going in the Army the same as the rest of the fellers. Ain't a conchie, are you?

Gran Alverstoke is good on conchies. Very tart about them. Straggling beards are a sign usually. Rhoda remembers hearing that they never have a decent bit of roast beef for Sunday dinner either. The real give-away – so Gran has told her – is sandals. There are those that are worse and they wear suede shoes. Rhoda has often tried to probe exactly why these are worse but has never been answered by more than a sniff and a pursing of the lips.

With what she feels to be a casual downward glance to inspect her own slippers, Rhoda assesses Harry's well-polished brogues. She feels reassured. When she looks up again Harry is smiling. Why shouldn't he? When he is eighteen there'll be nothing more than mopping up along the Under Den whatever it's called in Berlin. There seems to him to be no point at all in volunteering to mess up the doorway of some beer cellar with blood that already pulses to write poems. The world does not need a second Wilfred Owen.

–No. I'm not a conchie. But I've got . . . well, call it other plans.

Rhoda is as impressed – as he intends she should be. To her he doesn't compare too unfavourably with the late Leslie Howard. Not that Harry's face would be described in *Film Fortnightly* as sensitive. He lacks something of the chiselled gentlemanly features. Rhoda matches the vagueness of Harry's words against the role of Leslie Howard in *Pimpernel Smith*. It is a film she has seen twice. She also calls to mind a remark Alfie had once made about a country house near Brockenhurst in the New Forest.

–Secret stuff, is it? Special war work like?

–Not really. Just planning for the post-war world, actually.

–Sez you. Well, you would, wouldn't you? Secret agents have to be close about their work. Stands to reason.

Harry finds Rhoda amusing but he is beginning to feel hungry. He checks his wrist-watch to confirm that he must soon take a decision. Either to hang around in the hope that Mrs Blunt will return and offer him lunch or to scribble a note and make into town for a snack. He can be sure Rhoda will be able to direct him to a British Restaurant. Should there be a tiresome queue it would possibly leave time to get back – lunchless – and settle the matter of digs before keeping his appointment with the Senior Tutor.

–My name's Harry Plimsoll. What's yours?

–Me? I'm Rhoda.

–O.K. Any ideas where she may have gone, Rhoda? I think she was expecting me.

–She never said anything about a visitor. I expect she's at the shops. Or the library. She's a great reader. If her head's in a book, the bubble and squeak can burn itself black. There again, she could be meeting her brother. . .

–She's got a brother in Winchester?

–Thought you said your family knew her?

–Well . . . yes and no. My grandmother does. She told us they were great friends years ago. Anyway, she's got a brother here?

–Usually visits of a Thursday.

–This is Tuesday.

–Can't be him then, can it? You got a steady yet, Harry? A girlfriend?

–Sort of. . .

–Blonde is she?

–Good guess.

–Gran won't let me go blonde. Never trust a woman with fair hair, she always says. I shall go blonde, though. When I start earning at the factory for meself just let her try and stop me.

–Should make you popular with the Forces.

–'ere, what you mean? I'm spoken for already. I'm a decent person. Not that there's anything definite yet.

–And isn't he in the Forces?

–A driver in the Army, if you want to know. I could've brought his photo if I'd had warning. My Alf's blond. Got a cheery word for everyone, he has. He's a marvel with impressions, too.

–You mean he's a bit of an actor?

–Actor? Never. Gran wouldn't have it. You can never tell with theatre folk, she says. My Alf can do all the radio stars. And old Hitler. He's got Churchill off to a T. If I can trust you, I could tell you something else. . .

–Trust me.

You mustn't never let on. My Alf does a real killing take off of old No Better Than She Should Be. Her that lives here.

Harry ponders the implications of the name that Mrs Blunt has been awarded by at least some of her neighbours. It may be based on jealousy since houses further down the road are humbler. It may be that Vinnie had been trying to hint at something she's no wish that the rest of the family should know when she'd whispered that he might find Mrs Blunt would not be at all that he expected.

–It's a pity your Alf isn't about to entertain us with a curtain raiser.

–He could, too. What's more, he cooks better than she does. Gran encourages that. She says it'll leave me more time to attend to the babies.

–Going to have lots of children, are you?

–I'd like four. It's odd though. My Alf goes all funny whenever the conversation takes that turn. Hops out to the kitchen to make us a cuppa. I reckon he's shy. There's something refined in Alf. . .

As she speaks Rhoda's attention slips from her listener. Harry suspects she may be projecting herself forward a dozen years. May be trudging towards the shops with four children behind her. He decides that he will not confide in her that – a further four years on still – he could well be teaching them.

This is not Rhoda's daydream at all. It is true that Harry's face is of no more significance to her than a winter turnip. She is intent on conjuring up her Alfie's features and his stocky limbs. Even as she envisages them, they dissolve as images do in the films she sees. Just as Mr Hyde cross-fades to Dr Jeykll, her Alf becomes the young Charles Laughton. Quite as plump and twice as cuddly.

Harry gets up. Rhoda immediately does the same. She

tries to remember what she had been saying.

–'s funny, really. My Alf being refined and still just a driver. He's popular. Would you credit it? One of his officers takes him to see shows when they're up in London. That tells you how much Alf's appreciated . . . eh . . . look.

–Sorry, Rhoda. I'm going to have to go. . .

–Whatever for? I'm trying to tell you she's just come round the corner. That's her. Two spots of rain – no more than a kitten doing a tinkle – and she's got that old gamp of hers up. Bet you think it's to protect her clothes. You do then . . . don't you?

–All right. It's her hat she's worried about.

–Wrong. We knows what we knows. Something you London folks'd never click on to. I see her bedroom, don't I? Here. That's given you a clue.

–I'm still guessing. Has she just had her hair set or something?

–You just take a squint close to. Make up your own mind, of course, but I'm telling you that's a ginger wig. I've seen her spare one, see? Locked up in what she calls her hat-box.

And, with a triumphal smirk, Rhoda leads the way so that they form a welcoming party on the pavement. It occurs to Harry that Mrs Blunt may be short-sighted as well as bald for she gives no sign of noticing two teenagers by her gate. As he watches her negotiate the broken paving around a bomb site, Harry revises this impression. His potential landlady's progress has all the graciousness of royalty on newsreels combined with the fixed grimace of sweetness he has noticed on actresses who open Winifred's endless bazaars.

*

Would it be discourteous to enquire whether his landlady-designate is learning yoga in her retirement? Harry rather thinks it would. He suppresses a giggle as he studies her. Having related an involved anecdote that suggests his own grandmother was only marginally respectable in her youth, his hostess sits on the opposite side of her dining table with jauntily-painted eyelids closed. Occasionally they flutter, so indicating to Harry that life is not extinct. Her sherry glass is clipped between an extended thumb and forefinger while the remaining digits splay out like motionless antlers.

One might conjecture that elderly persons living alone tend to concentrate on memories of yesterday rather than on present happenings and such sensations as those – for example – that so occupy Harry Plimsoll. He glances around and waits to be rejoined in the here and now. His attention lingers on a sheaf of bulrushes in a jade green jar. He is sure Harding would consider them to be very phallic. To each bulrush tip a gaudy celluloid butterfly has been attached by a rubber sucker. Not in every instance – but in most – an artificial fly has been secured to the butterfly's wings. For a moment Harry regrets the vanity that precludes him from wearing his spectacles. He itches with curiosity. Are the tiny orange dots he perceives only a symptom of peering too long into the shadowy corners or are there, indeed, ladybirds perched on the flies?

Unable to confirm this, he becomes aware suddenly of the rightness of this ornamental set-piece. It could not fit as neatly in any other room. The very intricacy of it sums up the owner's manner of speaking. There is – Harry searches for the word – an adjective to describe such a style. He resolves to ask Hopalong Bentham and risk the tart response that sixth-formers should remember even a glancing reference in a lesson on style.

–Has it ever occurred to you, young man, that too much study can addle the brain?

–I'm sorry? I'm not sure what you're driving at.

–Nor I you. For the past hour – and for some reason best known to yourself – you have addressed me as Mrs Blunt. Are we agreed on that? Or has too much study, or too much family, reduced you to a gibbering half-wit?

–But, surely, you are Mrs Blunt, the respectable widow of

56

a canon at the cathedral?

–I am not Mrs Blunt and never have been. My name is Alice Violet Dowsett and I do not intend to change it. It might help us to discover the reason for this joke if you had another glass of sherry.

–Do you think I should? Might create a bad impression with the Senior Tutor. Wouldn't want him to think he might be taking on a young alcoholic.

–Balderdash. Vinnie and I used to drive out in a pony and trap to Emsworth when we were your age for a glass of ale and a sandwich. Never did us any harm . . . not the sort of thing to tell your sniffy mother. Or the appalling Winifred.

–You know, I can't imagine Grandmother Plimsoll getting up to a thing like that.

Miss Dowsett pauses as she refills the glasses. She emits a tiny breathless shriek and Harry is perturbed. What should he do if she is about to suffer a seizure? He feverishly recalls such First Aid lectures as he has attended at the Town Hall. None touched on the action Civil Defence Messengers should take when confronted with heart failures.

–Oh . . . you'll be the death of me, young Plimsoll. Oh . . . the heart. Too much excitement for one April day. First the new book on young Bess . . . then some charade in which I am cast as a clerical widow. Now this. Grandmother Plimsoll, indeed. Well, Vinnie can never say I didn't warn her. If you marry into that lot, I said, you'll get respectability like the rest of us get arthritis. Regular churchgoer now, is she?

–Yes, as a matter of fact. Evensong usually.

–Lorgnettes, too, no doubt and a bit of threadbare fox slung round her shoulders? It'll be Conservative garden parties next . . . if she hasn't succumbed already.

–So, what if she does know our local M.P.? She's always been kind to me. I've never thought of her as snobby.

–That may be something in her favour. Or in yours. I begin to see a possible reason for the invention of Mrs Blunt.

–Well, I don't.

–We'll come to that, Harry. Who's your local M.P.? Not one of my gentlemen, that's very certain.

As a second slice of apple tart is pushed at Harry, the throw-away line Miss Dowsett utters with a bronchial wheeze is not lost on him. If Miss Dowsett has – or has had – a retinue of gentlemen friends then Vinnie probably knows of it and has chosen to conceal it. As he pretends the sugar sifter has slipped – so making the apple tart almost palatable – he pursues the argument privately. Had his parents suspected that their son was to be the paying guest in a house of questionable repute, the whole college project would have foundered yet again. Vinnie has invented Mrs Blunt.

He can go no further into the whys and wherefores since Miss Dowsett expects some answer to her question. With his mouth conveniently full of apple tart, he finds he is beginning to shape a poem. More a satire. Miss Dowsett in retirement with, say, a distinguished public figure doing it against the sound of the Winchester cathedral bells. The title might be Evensong and the rhythm would need to be slow. The words would have to be chosen with some care. A succession of slurping sibilants. Harry swallows and answers briefly.

–Squadron Leader Keeling? He's our member. . .

The word amber might be useful in such a poem. Half rhymed with September? Harry feels that sombre should not be discarded. He regrets that Wilfred Owen would not be much help in such a composition.

–So dear Lavinia knows him. Better not call her Vinnie nowadays. . .

–Why not? The rest of the family does and I shall do in public when I'm twenty-one.

–I'm sure you will, dear. If the Great Reaper spares her. She had an energetic youth. More than one, if some of the tongues in Portsmouth wagged true. Not that I believe any of that. So unfair, don't you think, that you young gentlemen are expected to sow your oats, whereas we gels. . . ? Ah, well. Some coffee, Harry? I've only something called Camp in a bottle.

–Do you think I've time?

–Ten minutes walk, I'd say. You seem to have a stout pair of legs. Are you a virgin?

Having dabbed his mouth with a napkin not one minute since, Harry wipes it again vigorously. He's comforted to note that little sunshine filters through the heavy nets for he feels an instant flush rising from the back of his collar.

–Well, not exactly. I can assure you I'll not come creeping back at midnight with anybody in tow.

–Anybody? How very intriguing. Creeping back, you said? Most theatrical. Would that there were time to hear more. As a maiden lady I shouldn't, of course, wish to pry.

Harry stirs the fawn liquid silently. Despite her old world daffiness, there's a quaint salaciousness about Alice Dowsett that troubles him. He's no fears that she would steam open letters or inspect soiled bed linen. His unease is connected – in a tenuous way – with the ornamented bulrushes. It is possible Miss Dowsett might construct whole edifices of romance around people, too. If so – Harry reasons – what might she make of the most casual incident? A fellow student, for example, dropping round to return a book or to suggest a drink on a winter's evening? He has a lingering suspicion that Alice might begin with helpful advice and – within a term – be arranging his life for him. Like his Aunt Winifred, she appears to be a loner. If so, she might equal Winifred as a manipulator.

With not a sigh or a cough as preliminary warning, Miss Dowsett reopens her eyes and stares brightly at her guest.

–Before you go, do tell me about your grandmother's brother. Great-uncle Walter to you, no doubt. Vinnie is such a poor hand at letter writing these days. What's the news of Wallie?

–There isn't any, really. He's only a name to me. I think Aunt Winifred visits his wife in some Old People's Home. He was pretty vile to her, wasn't he?

–I know nothing of his wife. If he was vile to Winifred, it

would be justified.

–Oh, come on. You must know he was a drinker. Too far gone to put on a collar and tie when visitors were due for Sunday tea. . .

Miss Dowsett throws three heavily jewelled fingers to her throat. She chortles and despite the powder on her face, her features perceptibly begin to match her purple wallpaper. Harry is not alarmed. He gulps the remainder of his coffee and waits for her to speak.

–Oh, you're a wicked young buck to excite me with your jokes. Oh . . . the strain on the heart. Wallie Cosser a drinker? It's just as I thought. Vinnie's almost dead of respectability. I warned her against marrying that grandfather of yours. All flute-playing and water colours and lay preaching.

–I thought we were talking about Walter Cosser.

–Don't be snappish. Wallie was a founder member of the Communist Party. An amusing enough hobby and likely to remain so in this country. That was why he wouldn't put on ties for the would-be middle classes. At least he'd the courage to be himself.

–You astound me. I'd never heard that.

–And there's more you can hear whenever you take it into your head to come to Winchester and see me.

There's little point in Harry saying that Miss Dowsett has just astounded him a second time. Two over-full glasses of her sherry have scarcely been blotted up by a sketchy lunch. With each turn of the adroitly steered conversation, fresh and disturbing perspectives on his family have been disclosed. As he is about to rise from the table she pulls – as it were – the very linoleum from under him by inferring that he might not be suitable as a paying guest in her house.

Foremost in his mind is the urgent need for Miss Dowsett as an ally in his bid for independence. He decides to ignore the implication of her last remark.

–Just before I dash off to the College, I wonder if I might pop up and look at the room?

–Look at the. . .? What kind of suburban nonsense is that?

If you mean the jakes, say so. Or the W.C. . . . The room, indeed.

–Miss Dowsett, I mean the room I hope to have as a study . . . a bed-sitting room.

–Why in Heaven's name should you want one here?

As she speaks Miss Dowsett concentrates on repinning what Harry is, by now, quite sure cannot be her natural hair. A cascade of pins drops from the chestnut wig each time she secures one or other of the curls. She takes more notice of these than of Harry's agitation and he wonders if she might have been at the sherry decanter before her morning visit to the shops. He feels the tasteless fish cutlets rocking like a wherry at the base of his throat.

–But you must have had a letter from Vinnie. I'm sure she wrote to you. I'm hoping to be a student here in the autumn. You must help. Please, Miss Dowsett. Unless I can live with somebody the family trusts. . .

–You look as becoming as your own grandfather when you're agitated, young Harry . . . before he had aspirations to being a great gent that is. You'll break a heart soon enough. As yet I'm a little unsure. . .

–Miss Dowsett. Please. . .

–The situation does not arise, Harry. When I read Vinnie's letter. . .

–So you did receive it?

–Certainly. It was addressed to me. Not Mrs Blunt. So I made enquiries. My dear friend the librarian, Miss Fordingbridge, tells me the Teachers' College has been evacuated from Winchester since the beginning of this unfortunate difference we're having with Mr Hitler.

–Evacuated?

–That is what I said. The place is full of Army girls. Quite beautiful some of them are, too. Not that they have the frail pre-Raphaelite look of little Rhoda. Unfortunately she will chew American gum. Your college, Harry, is billeted somewhere rather remote. I believe Miss Fordingbridge mentioned Wales.

–Oh, dear God. Where?

–I can't recall whether it was North or South. Don't you agree they sing more lustily in the South?

–If you knew all this, why the hell didn't you say? Even if I do get a place here they'll probably not let me go to Wales. If I don't, it'll be too late to apply elsewhere. Oh crikey.

–Either way, you'll have to use persuasion or guile and what we'd once have called a bit of spunk to strike out for yourself. Vinnie managed it so I don't see why you shouldn't.

As she speaks Miss Dowsett smiles at Harry but he is absorbed in his own problem and is scarcely aware of the way his hostess is resettling a chiffon scarf to conceal the scragginess of her unpowdered neck.

–It's a challenge I could work out for myself, thanks. I begin to wonder why you even bothered to give me lunch. You could have told me all this at the door.

–But I wanted to discover why you should choose to address me as Mrs Blunt. Among other things. I now see that dear Vinnie was doing her best for you by inventing a canon's widow or whatever it was. You must see yourself as a resistance worker escaping from occupied territory, Harry. Mrs Blunt has brought you through hostile country to Winchester and. . .

–Yes, yes. Thank you very much. I shall have to dash.

Miss Dowsett does not rise from the table as Harry makes for the hall. He leaves the dining-room door open and their conversation concludes on a less than intimate level.

–Harry? I wondered if your grandma's gutsiness had been bred out in a couple of generations. It hasn't. That's your talisman and you'll need it with your unworldly father and your bullying mother. . .

–I'm sorry I'll not be staying here. Your rudeness is quite refreshing.

–Nothing you haven't already thought, I'll be bound. My love to Vinnie . . . and Harry? Harry?

–What is it? I'll be late.

–Say yes to whoever loves you first. *Whoever*, I said. . .

–Sounds a bit vague.

–Don't pretend to be a simpleton in my house. Do well at your interview.

With the graciousness of Queen Elizabeth – or perhaps a competent actress impersonating her – despatching a merchant venturer, Miss Dowsett waves Harry away. Winchester in April is not the Spanish Main. Harry Plimsoll does not burn with the certainty of his mission. By the time he has reached the Cathedral Close, however, his whole body glows and his raincoat billows out behind him. The fish cutlets rise mutinously in his gullet.

★

Within ten minutes Harry perceives that Dr Jocelyn Camford's interest in him has diminished remarkably. The Senior English Tutor's questions seem mechanical and his attention minimal. This contrasts remarkably with an eagerness so evident when he first glanced up from the fire to assess his potential student. Harry succumbs to an inner panic. Hasn't he done all in his power to make a good first impression? Whatever judgement Miss Dowsett might have voiced about his mother, Harry is forced to recall Margaret Plimsoll's insistence that it is the first impression that lasts.

While Dr Camford is recounting in a monotone the disadvantages of being evacuated to Wales with a bare two dozen students to keep the Winchester name alive, Harry re-enacts silently his first few moments in the spacious sitting room once the maid had closed the door behind him. He had remembered to leave both his faultlessly furled umbrella and his pork-pie hat on the hallstand inside the rather magnificent front door. If etiquette dictated that he should have handed them – together with his gabardine – to the maid, Dr Camford had not been there to note such a faux pas.

Jocelyn Camford is comparing the Welsh college unfavourably with even the north-western universities. Harry concentrates on what he has volunteered so far to the Senior Tutor that may account for a diminished interest.

It cannot have been the mention of poetry early on in their conversation. Harry had been most cautious in expressing too lively an interest. He wonders whether it might have been inappropriate to have enquired if dress for the evening meal was formal or semi-formal. To have mentioned that he would be packing his late cousin's black jacket and striped trousers would surely – he thinks – be no great gaffe.

Harry enumerates the points touched on in such conversation as there has been so far and Dr Camford's apparent reactions. One casual reference to the existence of Noreen had evinced a sympathetic nod. It had been only casual. To have stressed her as a serious involvement might have provoked a suspicion that the college could be enrolling a student whose mind would never be entirely on his work. On the other hand – Harry reasons – there would have been a greater hazard in keeping silent on the matter. At this point he gulps inaudibly but the Senior Tutor seems not to notice. Harry gulps because the thought rises unbidden that he might have mentioned nonchalantly his intention of sharing not just a night duty but a single bed with Joe within forty-eight hours.

As he begins to conjecture just what response there might have been to that observation, he realises that Dr Camford is peering at him expectantly. Some answer is required to a question of which Harry has heard little. More accurately, he recollects only the word music as being embedded somewhere in it.

–Music? Well . . . yes. The church choir until my voice broke.

–Since you name your Rural Dean as a referee I took that for granted. The musical tastes of parish organists invariably coincide with the generation before last. No doubt you sang Stainer and Parry from Christmas to Advent?

–Oh, yes. And Sullivan, too.

–Poor Sullivan. Such striving. But then . . . cockney son of an army bandmaster. Tell me . . . are you a cockney, Mr Plimsoll?

–Me? Not at all. We live twelve miles from the sound of Bow Bells.

–I was deceived. There seemed to be a lingering whiff of something under . . . what would it be? . . . Elocution lessons?

–Not really. I have been in school plays. I did once think of going on the stage.

–And what restrained you from the glamour of the footlights?

–To be honest, I don't see too well without these glasses. But I do have an uncle, actually, who has a small part in the film they're going to make of Shaw's *Caesar and Cleopatra*.

So Harry attempts to lead the conversation in a direction where he can enthuse and impress. It could be a reflected asset to be able to claim a relative on first-name terms with Claud Rains and Vivien Leigh.

Dr Camford certainly follows the lead.

–You read Shaw, then?

–Well, in a way. We've done *Pygmalion* at school.

–And you played Higgins?

–Actually, no. I was a cockney bystander in the first scene.

–Quite so, Mr Plimsoll. And what is your estimate of Shaw's social analysis? Is he sound, would you say?

–Oh, yes. I've read two or three of his Prefaces. I'm quite certain we'll need to change a lot of things in this country after the war . . . being a teacher, I would be able to play some part in that. . .

–In what, for instance?

–Well, I think it's terrible that poor families should have to trade their butter rations and sell these bottles of orange juice that are meant for their children. It's all going to the better off, while the poor exist on margarine.

–Interesting. And?

–Well . . . now I can look back on my Junior School days, I can see it was always all right for me. I was an obvious scholarship boy. But, well, I mean, there are plenty who were there with me who could be doing more than just humdrum jobs now . . . in wool shops . . . or as grocers' delivery boys.

–An admirable compassion. And who, then, would deliver the groceries?

–Well . . . I haven't really worked that one out. Maybe more people could have bicycles and carry their own weekend shopping. Or cars. Perhaps we'll all be able to afford cars when we've won.

–At least your zeal would not appear to motivated by spite. That's commendable. You've read Mr Wells?

–I remember seeing the film of *Things to Come*.

–No doubt. Mr Plimsoll, will you please tell me *one* book that you have actually read for pleasure rather than for examination. Just one.

–I rather like Smollett. The eighteenth century. . .

–I'm not unaware of his work. You don't find his texture somewhat coarse when compared with, say, Fielding?

–I haven't read Fielding.

–Not even *Tom Jones*, Mr Plimsoll?

–Well, I've seen the musical comedy adapted from it by Sir Edward German.

–Angels and ministers of grace defend us. Edward German. Sullivan in knee-breeches. The suburbs have much to answer for, Mr Plimsoll. Let us try once again. Who put you onto Smollett?

–My English master . . . Jeremy Bentham.

–Indeed. Some relative of the great utilitarian, now banished to the Thames Valley by the vicissitudes of war?

–Well, I believe his great something grandfather was a bit of a philosopher.

–You have a gift for understatement. Mr Plimsoll, I advise you to devote as many free hours as you can muster this summer to reading at your local library. Read, Mr Plimsoll. Read. In September we shall meet in Wales.

–You mean I'm accepted, Dr Camford?

–Are you about to decline the offer?

–Certainly not. But I do have one small problem.

The Senior Tutor heaves himself from the depths of a chintz-covered chair and stands with his back to the fire. Spring sunlight fondles the blue and white Dutch tiles on either side of him. Harry – also rising – is somewhat dazzled by the same light reflected in the overmantel. Additionally he is distracted by a curious sheen on Dr Camford's hair. Whatever the cause, the effect is startling. The Senior Tutor's hair is the colour of unripe lemons. Harry is so astounded by the coincidence of Miss Dowsett's wig and Jocelyn Camford's citrus tint in one day that he considers whether there may be material to hand for research. Would a university deem it too frivolous to commission a thesis on *Weird Wigs and Hair Tints in Mid-Twentieth Century Winchester?* Becoming absorbed by an image of himself in doctoral scarlet with perhaps a touch of dove grey at the throat and wrists, Harry almost fails to hear – for a second time – the question Dr Camford is putting to him.

–You have some antipathy to Welshmen?

–I don't recall ever having met any.

–You may find the experience enriching. There are indications that you've not succumbed entirely to suburban respectability. Like me, you may discover that many of these lads from the valleys have the simple appetites of shepherds.

–Shepherds? But they're miners' children, surely?

–Quite so. Separated from their idyllic hillsides merely by the accident of the Industrial Revolution. The Greeks could have been their cousins. Mr Plimsoll . . . is this object yours?

The pork-pie hat at which Dr Camford points is no longer the admired centre-piece of a High Street shop window. Seen through the Senior Tutor's eyes it is evidently a subject for mirth. Harry is sure that – given the option again – he would not choose to pool all his Christmas money to purchase it. For a few months it has been an outward sign that he has identified himself with Harding. Both nearly mature young men walking out with their girls on Sundays. One in a petrol blue pork-pie; the other in olive green. In the tiny silence before he speaks, Harry knows the hat will never make the journey to Wales.

–That? Oh . . . I borrowed it from a friend. There was rain threatening before I left this morning. Not the sort of thing I'd buy for myself.

–An umbrella would seem to be sufficient protection. Now – you have a problem?

–Well . . . yes and no. That is, I mean, I'll have to solve it. You see, there are moments when I actually wonder whether my parents resent my growing up. What I mean is – Dr Camford – Winchester would have been O.K. We have family friends here. Well . . . one. But if we're talking about Wales . . . it isn't exactly day-return country in wartime, is it? If they were keen to find out how I was living . . . like?

–My dear Mr Plimsoll, it is not for me to intrude into domestic grief. You must peck your own way out of the shell. Would your parents expect to accompany you on your honeymoon? Do you suppose they would wish to serve you cocoa and sandwiches on a landing barge should you have chosen to go straight to the Forces? If you wish to nourish what frail tendrils of personality are apparent in you, Mr Plimsoll, you'd best insist on a spot in the sun. I wish you well. . .

★

As he crosses the concourse at Waterloo Station, Harry repeats to himself – not for the first time within the past hour – his father's advice to relatives and neighbours who might chance to partner him at whist.

–*Never use a trump until you have to and then, for Gawd's sake, make it a big one.*

Threading between clusters of serving men and women who drink tea and wait for a train to Aldershot or Portsmouth, Harry silently mouths his father's advice again and again so that it becomes almost a talisman guiding him through the gloomy cavern of the terminus.

It is not until he has settled himself into the sour-smelling corner of an empty compartment that Harry evaluates the irony of using John Plimsoll's words to such a purpose as he has in mind.

For a couple of terms Harding has argued that, necessarily, there comes a moment when offspring must confront their parents. Alice Dowsett had waffled away over lunch about striking out for oneself. With a profusion of images, Dr Camford has endorsed Harry's increasing certainty that one need not necessarily experience only one birth but a succession of entrances into larger and wider worlds.

As the train crawls into each suburban station – barely identifiable by the frail blue light above its name-plate – Harry reconciles himself to another day ending in anguish and tears. He sighs and accepts this. Harding – already well read on pregnancies and childbirth – attests that pain cannot be excluded from a labour ward.

There is a moment of panic as Harry leaves the train. He is not so self-absorbed as to have hopped out at the wrong station. Nor is there anything apprehensive in his walk to the ticket barrier. The late duty porter does follow this solitary passenger's progress with interest for Harry alternately strides and gambols along the wooden platform. He plays both purposeful midwife and exuberant infant in his private birth drama. But the panic is quite another matter. At the barrier he turns to stare at the receding tail light of the train with horror. Only when the ticket collector is about to cough a second time does Harry recall he has left his pork-pie somewhere on the far side of Woking.

The knitted tea cosy twirls on Margaret Plimsoll's right hand like a glove puppet as she speaks. Although Harry listens to her, his interest is unevenly divided for he concentrates far more on the seemingly animated tea cosy. He follows what she says merely to check the predictability of her words and wonders whether she might have become a competent ventriloquist. Margaret's forefinger agitates the ornamental woollen forget-me-nots surmounting the cosy so that they seem to confirm – even though they do not voice – her comment.

–Why look at me, Harry? It's for your father to decide.

Her son restrains himself. His ace must be played later. Far too early in the game to waste it. He runs his hand through his hair and waits for his father to join in the conversation. John Plimsoll sighs noisily. He wishes it to be obvious that he resents having to put aside the crossword in his newspaper. He reaches for his packet of Craven A.

–Now, do we have to go through all this again? I made it plain, once and for all, that you could go in for this teaching business provided you'd be studying where someone we knew could keep an eye on you. Now did I or didn't I?

–You did, Father. Unfortunately, neither of us made the decision that the Army should commandeer the college in Winchester.

–Well, that's the end of it so far as I'm concerned. South Wales is absolutely out of the question. The Jerries have had a go often enough at Cardiff docks, haven't they? Who's to say they won't have a final fling?

–But, Father, Cardiff is South-east Wales. Steam coal from the valleys and with ready access to the Bristol Channel. . .

–You can cut that out. Your mother and I don't need Geography lessons. Where is this God-forsaken hole anyway?

–In the country beyond Swansea. I've just looked it up. No bombs. No industrial targets. It's farmland and it isn't God-forsaken. It's also run by the church not by the state.

–And teeming with miners' boys. I know a bit about the world, you know. And a darn sight more than you do about that crowd. Had to give them the push often enough at the Works and that's a fact. All beer and red hot unionism. More lip, too, than I get from you, which is saying something. Well, I don't know what to think . . . what do you say, my dear?

70

Margaret is stuffing tissue paper into the tea cosy to plump it up. She neither pauses nor looks up. To Harry, the object in his mother's lap now resembles an obese crinoline with a wizened torso. The forget-me-nots suggest to him the underdeveloped head and arms of a foetus such as Harding swears is kept locked away in a bell jar in every teaching hospital.

–Me? I've no thoughts on the subject. If you really do want me to pass a comment, I'm bound to say that all this college business has come as a shock to me.

–How so, my dear?

–Well, Harry can hardly say he's had his head in a book throughout the past two years. If he had then there might have been a scholarship to St Andrews or even Oxford. I could go on to name one of two around here who have managed such things . . . but . . . if I did . . . no doubt my son would tell me I'd be deriding him at the expense of strangers. He's your son, too, John and you must make the decision.

–And I'm your son, too, Mother.

–So you are. Now why should I sometimes think you overlook that?

–So, Father . . . what do you say?

Predictably to Harry, his father looks unhappy at having to make a decision. Not perhaps to Harry only. John Plimsoll's features are set in the kind of desolation many people exhibit when told of the death of a long-time friend or valued neighbour. He puckers his cheeks. He searches for comfort in the firelight. He wrings his hands.

–I'm forced to agree with your mother. There's been no sign until recently that you've any serious turn of mind. No sign at all.

–Father. At my age people change as quickly as the April weather. Surely you did? But in this I won't change again. I want to teach. I just don't understand all this fuss about money. You'll have to spend less on me than you do now. I'll get a loan from the County which I'll have to pay back. Not you. I'm sure the school will give me a Book Scholarship.

–And who'll be keeping you in the holidays, my laddie?

–At Christmas I'll work in the Post Office with the rest of the students, Mother. In the summer . . . I dunno . . . I could get a job on a farm over in Berkshire. . .

Margaret snorts with laughter and at last puts down the tea cosy.

–That'll please your father. Took his family three generations to get away from being farm hands and now you're proposing to run back to a pig-sty. Fat lot you know about anything practical. Can't even drive in a nail without bashing your thumb.

–Thank you for the vote of confidence, Mother. Shall we talk about your family while we're at it?

–Less of that. Don't go upsetting your mother. I'm bound to say I'm not too keen on this Welsh lark at all. I think we should forget it. Now look, Harry. I'll have a word at the Works tomorrow with our Drawing Office. If we can get you in there you'd have a trade behind you when the time comes for you to be called up. It would stand you in good stead. . .

Harry tries to stop himself sweating. Time to play the ace. He knows his father is out of court cards and has nothing but throwaways in his hand.

–I know the offer's kindly meant but . . . no thanks.

–If you imagine, my boy, that when you've left school in a couple of months you're going to lounge around this house all day, expecting your father to keep you and me to wait on you, you've got another think coming. You should have had my mother.

–Can I finish what I was going to say, please?

–Whatever it is, make it snappy and make it convincing. Your father's got no pension to look forward to and we need to put something away for our old age. We're not likely to get fat waiting for any help from you in that direction.

–Thank you. Now. Although I'm not quite old enough to be hanged I am old enough to go into the Army. Hold on, please. I know they won't call me up until I'm eighteen but they do accept volunteers. . .

–Blackmail now, is it? I should have guessed. Assert yourself, John. We don't have to listen to this twaddle.

–Don't go getting yourself into a state, my dear. He's had no time to go to Winchester and nip into Kingston Barracks as well.

–Father, I had no need. The Light Infantry is based at Winchester, as you'll have noticed when you visited Grandmother before I was born. When I passed the gates. . .

–Don't try your acting nonsense on your father. You go to a barracks? It surprises me you had the guts. . .

–But you're wrong. I do have the guts. The Army makes a man of you but the Hampshire Light Infantry makes you a hero. Isn't that what they say, Father? The only regiment that marches at a hundred and sixty paces to the minute? Right?

–I believe I've heard something to that effect. Harry . . . for goodness sake . . . what on earth do you want to go and do a thing like that for? You won't even be seventeen until the summer.

–Because . . . if I can't go to college I don't intend to lounge about anywhere. Least of all here. With any luck at all I suppose I won't get shot before the Armistice. If I come through I shall have saved my pay and then I can go straight on to college. I might even learn some Welsh between the Infantry charges.

John Plimsoll looks as though he might weep openly at any moment. He lights another cigarette and suggests – after blowing his nose – that the cat might need to be let out into the garden. Margaret gets up silently and places her tea cosy on an occasional table. She snaps the clasp of her knitting bag and leaves it by the chair.

–I am going to bed. Let me know in the morning what decision you come to and just what part I have to play in your plans. Goodnight.

★

73

Margaret knows Harry's light step on the stairs well enough. She misconstrues his intention of not waking her for a wish to avoid any further interchange on college or National Service. He passes her door and is already on the way to the second storey when she appears from her darkened bedroom.

—A word with you, young man. You may think you've got round your father with that nimble tongue of yours. I'm not deceived. You knew very well there was no college at Winchester, didn't you?

—If that's what you want to think, Mother, I can't make you do otherwise. . .

—It doesn't take degrees and diplomas to work out that grandmother of yours let you know all about it on the quiet and still persisted in egging you on. She would, of course. Just to spite me.

—Grandmother Plimsoll told me nothing other than you already know. I had an introduction to Mrs Blunt in Wessex Avenue. You saw the piece of paper for yourself.

Both of them hear the downstairs lavatory door close behind John Plimsoll. He will remain there for fifteen minutes and then pull the chain. He will then walk into the hall leaving the lavatory door ajar to allow the cigarette smoke to disperse. Margaret would like to use that quarter of an hour to discover whatever it is she is convinced that Harry is concealing. He is genuinely tired and has no intention of provoking yet another row by disclosing that Mrs Blunt was and will be a fabrication.

—So, what did Mrs Blunt give you to eat?

—Fish cutlets and apple tart. Both delicious.

—You amaze me. Most of Vinnie's friends are such gadabouts they never seemed to have the time for anything more than a quick fry-up.

—Mrs Blunt must be the exception. As you know she's a canon's widow so it's a very quiet house. She has some help in the mornings, like you.

—Pity you won't be going, then.

—Yes.

74

–That all you can say for yourself or do I have to drag it out of your father? What's been decided?

–Once I know I've got a place – in writing that is – I expect the next step is fixing the loan and money from school and that's it.

–Well, it had better be. You'll not be getting a degree of course from this place?

–No. But you can tell your friends I'll be getting a diploma. The degree can come later. Evening classes. . .

–You'll never put your mind to that. Like the rest of your father's family you'll be frittering your time and energy on parties and theatricals. Out and spending, that's their motto.

–Mother. You could be wrong, you know. I know they wouldn't let you be a teacher. Do try and accept that letting me be one is the next best thing. Goodnight.

Harry is asleep within ten minutes and John within thirty. It is midnight by Margaret's bedside clock when she turns on the light again to reread an article on redecorating conservatories during wartime in *My Home*.

★

Harry rests the back of his neck against the white enamelled lip of the bath. On a cloudless evening in May he finds it a not unpleasant sensation. In five minutes – ten at the very most – the bath water will have become unpleasantly tepid and he will need to soap himself. Until then he can – and does – stare at the sky through an open dormer window, listening to sounds that drift from gardens and kitchens below.

By wriggling his knees in a restricted dog paddle, Harry can swirl the seven inches of water he allows himself to a tolerable warmth. Government advertisements suggest that in the interests of the war effort only five inches should be used. Harry has long since reconciled his conscience to exceeding this limit. The advertisements do not specify hot or cold water or a blend of the two. To five inches of boiling water from the zinc heater he adds two from the cold tap. On this particular evening in May it occurs to him that there have been no instances in the local papers of people arrested for unpatriotic behaviour. Neither is it likely his parents with their post-Victorian prudery – swathed in a pretended respect for individual privacy – will attempt to intrude or remonstrate. At most Harry can expect a yell from the landing below reminding him that there are others who might like a Friday-night bath before midnight.

Even that is improbable. John Plimsoll is busy setting out tomato plants he has bought in East Lane market. Margaret has gone with a neighbour to a cookery class in the parish hall. Harry becomes aware that his cock is rising and he stares at it with a frown. He can think of no logical reason for it to do so. The cooling water lapping his genitals in no way resembles the roughened stubby fingers that will close on his flesh the following Monday night in some draughty school gymnasium. The formulation of this comparison serves only to strengthen the blood pumping into the shaft of his cock. Harry is fascinated that his conscious thought of tomato plants and cookery classes should prompt an erection. It is like an unbidden poem popping up during lunch at Alice Dowsett's.

He dismisses the thought of a quick wank. It would have seemed to him an adequate solution at thirteen. He wonders how fellow sixth-formers are coping with their sex problems. One or two hint that their steady girlfriends are prepared to offer a quick bit of relief in the fields across the river. He is sure that Harding and Sue Naylor have gone all the way. Once or twice, when cycling home, Harding has asked knowingly how it's going on a physical level with Noreen. Harry has replied with a shrug and an assurance that he has no need to get his satisfaction by sticking it into a piece of raw liver or between a couple of greased dining plates. This earthiness has appealed to Harding just as Harry hoped and the matter hasn't been raised again for weeks.

None of this eases his erection. With a determination moralists would applaud, he concentrates on the least erotic image that's available at short notice: that of the Plimsolls' grossly eccentric neighbour. Through the open dormer he can hear Miss Griffith's voice braying at his father. The words are enunciated carefully, with a certain hollow quality that Harry begins to associate with the slightly deaf.

–Life is no longer very pleasant for a gentlewoman, Mr Plimsoll. I'm only glad I've no children and I'd like to think you're looking after the welfare of that lad of yours. We've some most unsavoury characters lurking about in what my grandfather termed a delightful backwater. Only the other evening, Mr Plimsoll, I was perusing my evening paper in the twilight by the entrance to the Public Baths. I just happened to glance up and there, under the chestnut trees, was a person playing with himself.

Harry giggles at the euphemism and so does not hear his father's comment. If any. His own delight is redoubled as he looks down to confirm that his cock is now floating like an uncooked sausage in a horsehair pool.

Grabbing at a towel, he leaps from the bath and, with rivulets from his limbs seeping across the linoleum, inspects crevices on either side of his nostrils in the mirror. He has become aware of a new teenage hazard: blackheads. In removing them, he inclines to the squeezing technique, rather than tugging at the skin until tiny worms of coagulated grease and soap appear.

While harvesting the weekly crop, Harry repeats Miss Griffith's last phrase and, as he does so, wriggles his shoulders in a blend of outrage and delight. This is resolved to unalloyed pleasure as the mirror's reflection shows two hairs on his chest. Only the grandfather clock striking seven two floors below disrupts his fascination.

–Shit and derision.

With the speed of an experienced actor in a bedroom farce, he throws on his clothes. In less than two minutes he is tugging at the knot of his new tartan tie. It is not clan McCawdie. Possibly no clan at all. The background is egg-yolk yellow on which violent bands of scarlet and green are criss-crossed. Studying the effect, even Harry has reservations. He dismisses these with the justification that, if one is to become involved with the arts, there's little point in being taken for an apprentice bank clerk.

Hearing his father shouting from the hall below, Harry opens the bathroom door.

–I said, are you going to this darned show at the Town Hall or not?

–Just coming, Father. It doesn't start till eight.

Taking the stairs three at a time, he steers round John Plimsoll with arms outstretched in his Spitfire imitation before dumping dirty socks and relatively unsmeared pants in a wickerwork basket below the kitchen sink. When he returns to the hall he finds his father still in front of the mirror. Harry peers quickly to either side for a final check on his appearance.

–Good God alive. What kind of a get-up d'you call that?

No longer stung by his parents' mockery of anyone who, through personal preference, deviates from suburban convention, Harry concentrates on checking his pockets as he answers.

–I'm off to a poetry reading, not a parade of the Light Infantry in Winchester, Father.

He taps his street-door key before fingering the ten-shilling note that will cover two tickets and a shandy for Noreen and himself either during the interval or, later, at the Waterman's.

–Well, you do look a sight and no mistake. Poetry readings? We've had no decent poets since Kipling. . .

–Since he's dead we just have to put up with the living.

–Less of your lip. And why do you have to go on mucking about with that hair of yours? Always pushing it this way and that like some spiv in a market. As for that darned tie . . . the sooner you're in the Army the better, and no mistake. Anyone'd think you wanted to be taken for a nancy boy. . .

Harry opens the street door. At the front gate he undoes his lovat sports jacket to treat the world to a glimpse of his sky-blue Van Heusen shirt and clan McFantasy tie. Once on the pavement he calls back to his father.

–I'm not even sure what a nancy boy is. Like most other things, I suppose I shall have to find out for myself. See you in the morning. . .

–Now don't come wandering home here at all hours. Just remember you're not twenty-one yet. There could be a raid, you know. And don't expect me to sit up until midnight.

–I'll be in about half eleven, I expect.

–The place'll be full by the time you get there. All behind, as usual, like the cow's tail.

–We'll find seats. It's only poetry after all, Father.

As he waits for the bus, Harry realises that his father's taunt about his hair has stung. Only by coating it as thick as a layer of paint with Brylcreem can even one hint of a wave be coaxed into it. He envies Harding and other sixth-formers – Joe too – who have natural curls and waves. Not for the first time he wonders whether he could live with wolf whistles along the High Street were he to have a perm. It would call for almost V.C. courage. Harding had been catcalled as they'd left the Waterman's simply for wearing a pair of suedes. True, Harry recalls, Harding's reply had been a couple of nifty uppercuts. There had been no further catcalls at the Waterman's. Harry makes a mental note to add a pair of suedes to his college shopping list.

By angling his head to a point at which he risks straining his neck muscles, Harry can catch his reflection in the window of the bus. Preoccupation with his hair continues. There is, at least, plenty of it and he feels he can trust Harding's rule of thumb analysis: to assess any danger of baldness one should study one's mother's brothers. Neither of Harry's McCawdie uncles is even sparse on top.

*

The hall in which the poetry reading is to be given is joined to the main civic building. A nineteenth-century addition not out of keeping with the seventeenth-century

79

mansion in which two British monarchs had been born. Harry sprints from the main gates and is irritated to discover Noreen is not waiting for him. Nor is there any sign of Harding or Sue among the borough's intelligentsia straggling into the side entrance. It is ten minutes to eight.

During the five minutes he decides to allow his friends, Harry has ample time to study the sleek black Rolls parked in front of the Town Hall's main entrance. He knows it is not the Mayor's so he deduces it must be – together with the chauffeur – the property of the readers. Ergo there must be money in poetry. Having circled the flower-bed to which the drive from the gates leads, yet still having not caught sight of his friends, he reconsiders the car. This time he concedes perhaps the money it cost preceded the poetry. An assured income might have begotten the leisure that begat the inspiration that led to the poetry. This thought doesn't prompt in Harry any pointless envy. He wonders, instead, whether it might be that his whole family is concealing from him a tremendous secret. Will they – on his twenty-first birthday – reveal that he is no blood relative at all? That he was adopted on condition his entitlement to an income and a villa somewhere up the river should not be revealed until his coming of age? He visualises them surrounding him – Vinnie with what she habitually refers to as *good-hearted tears* in her eyes – explaining that all the tiresome privations have been for his own betterment. A sort of character assault course to guarantee his fitness to manage complicated stocks and shares. Only the church clock beginning to strike eight brings him down. One glance towards the main road confirms that he will be attending the poetry reading without his friends. A second – at his pocket mirror – confirms that he is very certainly his parents' son.

He pays for two tickets and leaves one with Noreen's name scribbled on it at the door. The hall is very full and it is an increasingly irritated Harry Plimsoll who scurries towards the front at a minute past eight. He is in no mood to listen to explanations from Noreen or Harding, for it is on them that he blames the likelihood that he'll have to stand at the back. About to do just that, he spots a seat in the seventh row with a raincoat thrown over it. It seems worth asking whether it is being reserved for a latecomer like himself.

–Excuse me. . .

A man in his mid-twenties looks towards Harry with slightly raised eyebrows. Not a forbidding face. With seconds to go before the performance must start, Harry still has time to register a mop of brownish curls and envy them.

–That seat taken?

–I was expecting somebody but he's obviously not going to make it. You're very welcome.

The voice is flatter than the Thames Valley and unlike the Winchester accent that every rustic on the wireless seems to imitate. As Harry pushes past half a dozen pairs of knees he happens to glance back towards the door. There is a chance that Noreen may have arrived. She has not but his attention is diverted by Harding and Sue waving happily at him a few rows back. Harry bares his teeth at them in a savage grimace and sits down.

–Are you local?

–Eh? Oh yes. Yes, I know this place very well.

The chatter around him subsides and there is a clearing of throats. The stage lighting is full and harsh against the black wartime backdrop. This contrasts and highlights a graceful antique table which, Harry guesses, is usually in the Mayor's parlour and two vast baskets of early roses.

Applause begins at the front rows and sweeps back over Harry strong as waves he recalls as a child surging towards him over the Portsmouth shingle. The two poets move confidently from the wings to stage centre. Harry has prepared himself for something dramatic. The woman who stands bowing graciously to her capacity audience plays no one but herself. To Harry she appears immensely tall and it crosses his mind that she may wear what actors call lifts to increase her height. If this does not account for her statuesque appearance then it has to be the full-length

81

robes she wears. Clothes would be a totally inadequate noun. Harry tries a rough estimate of the number of clothing coupons that must have gone into her grass-green gown that touches the stage itself. Refusing to associate a distinguished writer with the black market, he still does wonder how one could obtain the cloth of gold cope. Either she had sent the chauffeur to rob a bishop's wardrobe or – Harry feels it more probable – like poor Scarlett O'Hara during another war, she'd torn down the casement curtains and run up the cope one wet afternoon when inspiration had been at a low ebb. Round her neck hangs what history-book illustrations have taught him is an SS chain. The writer could have inherited one. Harry's mother has told him the woman is of noble family. It might have been hired from a theatrical costumier. There is what Joe calls an outside chance that the ornament may have been knocked up for her by a village blacksmith.

There's no telling her age. Harry is content that this should be so. One of his Junior School teachers had always asserted that poetry should be timeless. Whatever hair she may or may not have is concealed under a toque of silver lamé from which great tongues of the same material extend. There is more than a vague similarity – or so Harry thinks – to the head of Medusa as illustrated in Latin Today (Book One). Her face is powdered white and Harry is thankful that Vinnie is not beside him. Undoubtedly she'd whisper – none too softly – that the poet had been at the flour bag again. Her eyelids as well as her lip and fingernails are much the colour of a freshly chopped beetroot.

Only when she produces her reading glasses can Harry link her with wartime England. These are pink-rimmed. Even to distinguished poets, beetroot frames might be unobtainable in wartime.

As she begins to flick through her foolscap manuscript book, Alderman Daisy, who chairs the Arts Committee, begins a simple but rather obvious speech.

The male poet certainly frets at the lengthy introduction. He fidgets in one of Aunt Winifred's three hideous nineteenth-century carver chairs loaned for the performance. He unbuttons his dinner jacket and then rebuttons it. Almost noiselessly he taps the boards with his stick. Harry suspects the man may have been wounded in the First World War. He can be certain the man did serve on the Western Front. After two hours in the school library he remembers this and just one impressive line . . . *the port wine coloured gentry*. Harry giggles silently. It is as though the poet had written that line while staring into his shaving mirror. He wonders whether he should tease his mother by telling her of the baronet with the port wine chops. It would be hardly likely to diminish her reverence for the gentry.

At last Alderman Daisy flutters her podgy jewelled fingers to the visitors.

–. . . and so, with very great pleasure, I will ask Miss Edith and Sir Osbert Sitwell to read to us.

She sits but neither of the poets stands. Sir Osbert enquires loudly of the audience whether it is aware of the evening's programme. Harry and his neighbour join in shouts of No around the hall. There's a mild nervous laughter from those who do not think it nice to shout at the aristocracy. Harry and his neighbour exchange smiles.

Sir Osbert seems genuinely astonished.

–Then I shall acquaint you with it. My sister will read for fifteen minutes and then I shall read for fifteen minutes. My sister will resume and read for a further ten minutes after which I shall do the same. We shall then require some refreshment. Arrangements have presumably been made for you as well. After a thirty-minute interval my sister will read to you for ten minutes and I shall do likewise. The evening will conclude with a further fifteen minutes of my sister's poems and our car will be waiting to leave at ten o'clock.

There is no protest from the audience. After nearly five years of being directed by street wardens and regulated by ration books it accepts, without one murmur, the plan of campaign outlined by Sir Osbert. Harry puts his head down to giggle into his handkerchief and wonders whether there might be other odd pockets of dissent around the hall. When he does raise his head he finds his neighbour is controlling his amusement by biting his lower lip. He whispers to Harry in an accent that reminds the younger man of one of the northern newsreaders, taken on to convince radio listeners that the war is nationwide.

–As if we couldn't guess that old bugger was in the last lot. Straight in as an officer, needless to say. . .

–I looked him up in the library. A friend of Owen and Sassoon, too. . .

–Ssshhh. . .

A woman in a Breton sailor hat – patriotic navy, piped with crimson and white cord – hisses but does not bother to turn her head. With the advantage of two hours in the library behind him, Harry wonders how much the woman might understand of the poems which are about to be read. Edith Sitwell rises as her brother concludes.

–My sister, as you observe, stands to read her work. I trust I shall be excused if I remain seated. My gout is troublesome at present.

Harry attributes this to an over-indulgence in port.

The darkened hall is soon transformed for Harry to an art gallery in which all his attention becomes pinpointed on the reader. The yellow roses beside her turn to beaten gold and the scarlet blooms transmute to miniature versions of the sun that stares at him on summer afternoons when he lies with eyes half shut. For minutes on end, the black drapes on the stage recede and Edith Sitwell's words furnish the space around her with fabulous beasts and story-book characters that dart and scurry from her ornate cope.

And then – as she pauses between two poems – Harry hears a door bang somewhere beyond the hall. When she resumes he sits back and folds his arms. The world which she outlines and then colours and offers to her audience touches him only if he concentrates on his childhood. He listens for the sound of the sirens weaving through the lines but it is not there. The old Movietone shot of

Chamberlain at the aerodrome with his piece of paper replays itself as Harry closes his eyes but the reader speaks of the morning light creaking down again.

He will never be sure how long he dozed or whether the woman in the sailor hat dozed or what Sir Osbert read during the first part of the programme. Perhaps Edith Sitwell worked on him like a fairground hypnotist. When she begins again she sways as though she may have hypnotised herself a little. Within seconds Harry revises his previous opinion of her. She *is* aware of the torn world in which her audience is struggling to live. The rain she speaks of is the rain of shrapnel and small incendiaries that spatters on the High Street and the factories and the back gardens. It is the fire of doodlebugs drifting in the wind over slums and hospitals. The rain that may intensify to one last terrible storm as the Allied armies sweep across France and towards Berlin.

Still falls the Rain
At the feet of the Starved Man hung upon the Cross.
Christ that each day, each night, nails there, have
     mercy on us –
On Dives and on Lazarus:
Under the Rain the sore and the gold are as one.

One reservation lingers in Harry's mind. If only the woman wouldn't recite with such an affected BBC accent. If only she and Frank Phillips and Alvar Liddell and Stuart Hibberd wouldn't lengthen their vowels to speak of crawss and lawss. Yet, despite this, and despite Harry's contempt for all references to tiresome Christian teachings that concentrate on suffering and death, he – and his neighbour – join in the ovation which the poem receives.

*

–How do you feel about a cup of coffee? Don't expect there's a bar.
–Well . . . no thanks. Actually, I've got to nip out and see a friend of mine who's with his girl. Promise I will be

85

back for the second half though. Keep the seat for me, will you?

★

–Now don't start, Plimsoll. Sue and I both saw you give us your Englisher swinehund look as you sat down. You were late and we waited until nearly ten to.
–So where the hell's Noreen?
–Harry. If you'll calm down and listen. . .
–Well . . . where is she? I bought her a ticket. . .
–We called for her on the way. Harding waited downstairs and I went up to see her. Nothing serious. Just . . . a bit of woman's trouble.
–What woman's trouble?
–As your medical adviser H.P., I have to say use your common and look at the calendar.
–Eh? Oh . . . Oh, I see. Well, couldn't she have told me yesterday?
–Perhaps she didn't know yesterday. Hoped this evening might be O.K. Anyway . . . what d'you think of the show? Sue and I were saying it's more your line of country than ours. Gives us a chance to hold hands in the dark though. . .
–Really, Harding. You've the soul of a surgeon already. I'm not sure whether I can get serious about you.
–D'you hear that, H. Plimsoll? I sit for hours with her, innocently planning a new semi out in the Green Belt for when this is all over . . . nice village local to entertain you and Noreen – when you've got the fare. And now? Now she's having doubts. Not like Noreen, eh? Bet she's got one hundred per cent trust in you. . .
–Yes . . . well . . . I'll think about domestic joy in the suburbs in another ten years, maybe. Meanwhile, can I offer you both a half in the Waterman's afterwards?
For a moment, Sue looks at Harry with bewilderment. She drops her glance, still considering what he has just said, and nudges Harding with her shoulder.
–We could, couldn't we? Harry's by himself, after all.

86

–True. On the other hand, I'm sure he's some work to do. As for us, honey-bun, we might take a stroll under the willows.

–Just so long as you keep it to that, Mr Octopus.

–O.K., you two, see you soon. Like tomorrow, Harding?

★

A path of York paving stones leads, from beyond the tennis courts, among scarlet and white rose beds to the sunken garden. There are no visitors other than Harry Plimsoll who perches himself on the base of a broken plinth. With his face cupped in his hands, he appears to be staring at the back elevation of the Town Hall. Were a platoon of German parachutists to creep silently in front of the facade, it's unlikely that he'd notice anything untoward.

He broods less on Harding than on Noreen. His friendship with Paul – P.H., as Harry increasingly thinks of him – is cooling into something of a ritual.

The closeness that had seemed to exist until the beginning of the year means progressively less to Harry. Paradoxically, Harding appears more matey as his relationship with Sue Naylor absorbs more of his free time. To Harry, there is now no question of reopening discussions about post-war travel. Maps over which they once pored – on which lines between Paris and Rome and even Athens had been drawn – could be rolled up as others had been in 1914.

Not that Harry himself abandons the plans. It does cross his mind that, should Harding broach the subject, inevitably Sue would figure in it. This – Harry reasons – would just as inevitably lead on to the inclusion of Noreen in a roving quartet. It is a plan that Harry rejects. He fears he would be out-manoeuvred. The likelihood of seeing and doing what he would wish to see and do would inevitably be diminished to a one in three chance. The betting phrase evokes Joe Gibbs. Harry wonders whether he has too readily allowed Harding's place as the ideal travelling friend to be taken by Joe because the latter can be more easily led. This he dismisses. Joe has an independence not quickly swayed. As for initiative – Harry recalls the instances in which Joe has first suggested cycling down unmarked lanes.

A bat, swooping through a clump of poplars in the dusk, distracts him for a moment. He recalls, almost with horror, the brief interchange he had with Harding and Sue as the interval began. To be planning a house complete with electricity bills and dirty nappies while still wearing a school blazer seems ludicrous. It is possible – or so Harry at this moment supposes – that Noreen has been waiting for him to talk less of writing and travel and more of saving to become established in the community. He repeats the phrase he has heard his mother use and convinces himself that his irritation is justified. The only rebuttal he can call to mind is Wilfred Owen's irony *Was it for this the clay grew tall?* To sixteen-and-three-quarter-year-old Harry Plimsoll, the phrase is relevant not only to a dead soldier in a French field. Without the option to grow and to become oneself one might as well – he feels – forget college and poetry and make for Kingston Barracks.

Five mornings a week on a suburban train, he thinks, followed by Saturday jobs around the house and the Sunday treat of lunch with the in-laws can be seen as nothing other than a bullet in slow motion trained to embed itself imperceptibly below the fifth rib.

If that is to be the price exacted in return for a cuddle with Noreen, it is too high for Harry to pay. He is about to sketch out an acceptably cool argument that must be put to Noreen, when a moth touches his cheek. In brushing it aside he notices his watch.

–Shit and derision.

He shakes his watch. The hands are not whirling like a Hurricane out of control.

Of course the second half of the programme has been under way some time before he has sprinted back to the side entrance of the hall. He knows there is no question of sidling along the aisle while Sir Osbert is rumbling on. It is

odds on that his seat has been taken. From the back he tries twice – and fails – to count the shadowy heads in search of the row in which he was sitting. At the third attempt, he spots the woman in the Breton sailor hat. There is a gap behind her. During the applause which follows Sir Osbert's final poem, Harry darts swiftly before Edith Sitwell rises to conclude the evening's entertainment. The young man looks up and smiles while removing his raincoat.
–Thanks.
–Thought you'd had enough.
–No . . . I was talking to friends. . .
–And are you drinking with them too? Later, like?
The Breton sailor hat in front of them rotates a mere two degrees to NNE but the sound emitted from beneath is as piercing as a sudden gust from due north.
–SSSHHH.

*

–So who's the other old biddie? The one with the stick who was sitting in the middle?
–Chairman of the Education and Arts Committee for the borough.
–Have they all got gout round here from black-market booze?
–Shouldn't think Alderman Daisy has. I think she told us it's arthritis.
–Well in with her, are you?
–She's a pal of my social aunt. . .
–And does that make you a pampered child of the bourgeoisie?
–Ummm . . . well I don't think I am.
–*Would* you mind? We are *all* trying to get out. . .
In response to the pained request from the woman in the Breton sailor hat, Harry stands aside. This interruption in the conversation does allow him to rack his memory for an exact meaning of the word bourgeoisie. He wonders whether he might have misheard. Could his neighbour's

accented voice have said *bergeroisie* which might have a
connection with the French noun for shepherd? Before
he has a moment to dismiss this as unlikely, since the
last flocks disappeared from the borough at the turn of
the century, he finds himself at the edge of the gravel
driveway outside. Not far from him an assorted cluster
of admirers surrounds the Sitwells' Rolls. His neighbour
interposes himself between Harry and the fan club.

–The name's Tony. Tony Ackers. What's yours?

–Me? I'm Harry Plimsoll. As in gym shoes.

–Might account for your bounce. So what's this Alderman Daisy expected to do for you? Did you come for the
poetry or to be seen by her?

–For the poetry, of course. I'm going to be an English
teacher, you see. You never know, though. Old Daisy
might come in useful. . .

–That's what it's about then? Making use of people?

–No. No, of course not. I liked the poetry. Well . . . some
of it. . .

–And it could come in useful as you're going to teach
English?

–Hey . . . why are you trying to get at me all the time?

–I'm not. Just interested in the way people tick. Fancy a
coffee, Harry?

–Oh, I don't know about that. Time's getting on. . .

–I'm a teacher, too. English as it happens. I work just over
the river. . .

–Do you? Well I suppose coffee wouldn't be a bad. . . Shit
and derision.

–Now what's your problem?

–My social aunt. The one bearing down on us in full sail.
There's no escape, Tony.

Winifred Plimsoll, neé Hornbeam, trots towards them as
fast as her calf-length fur coat will permit. She wears a
silk square knotted at the point of her chin. The effect
is unhappy. The scarf accentuates the grimness of her
features. It emphasises her fleshless nose and chin. Her
arrival is signalled – as it usually is – by a jangle of
bracelets that Harry likens to a leper's bell.

–Hello, Harry dear. You'll have enjoyed it all of course being the bookish one of the family. Bit beyond me, I'm afraid. . .

–Aunt Winifred, this is Mr Ackers. He teaches English at the Grammar School across the bridge.

–Nice to meet you. I'm Harry's aunt. I'm not a Plimsoll by birth. One of the Sussex Hornbeams.

–I'm afraid Harry didn't get my credentials exactly right, Mrs Plimsoll. I teach at the orphanage on the hill. . .

–The place I pass on my way to the Star and Garter? Wasn't that the ragged school years ago? I suppose it's quite respectable now. We must all muck in, mustn't we? Did I tell you I'm on the Committee now for the Poppy Day appeal, Harry? Lady Shrinknees and I were elected last week. . .

–Isn't she the one Grandmother says was a chorus girl and no better than she should be?

–Oh no, dear. Old Vinnie gets confused you know. Now – where are you two boys off to? Not many pretty girls about tonight, are there? All a bit like that old frump on the stage. I said to Daisy that Miss Sitwell could stand in at Madam Twoswords and no one would know the difference. . .

–Will you be going straight home, Aunt Winifred?

–Oh I expect so, dear. They may announce the second front on the radio at any time. Your uncle and I wouldn't want to miss that.

–Would you mind phoning Father or Mother for me? Tell them I'm off to hear about teaching first-hand from Tony. Mr Ackers. I've got my key. They needn't sit up.

–Very well, dear. Ah . . . there's Daisy and Sir Osbert now. I must just go and tell him how much I enjoyed his little verses. Nice to have seen you, Mr Ackers. . .

–Will she telephone do you think?

–Dunno. Don't much care.

*

The young soldier is not at all displeasing. Margaret bases this judgement on his bearing as he stands half a

91

minute away from her by the gates of the West Middlesex Hospital. There is something – perhaps not only the angle at which he holds his head but the effect of the sunset on his tanned features – that recalls for her a young officer on the *Kilimanjaro* when she had first sailed for Mombasa. Not that the young serviceman obviously waiting for one of the nurses to come off shift would be likely – or so Margaret assumes – to have quite the class of an officer. She wonders whether she might be unfair and hasty in this conclusion. His *Good Evening Ma'am* as he passed the bus stop was pleasing enough and the accent was softer than that of a Chicago gangster with a mouth full of gum. She guesses – correctly – that he is Canadian.

She forgets the soldier as the bus approaches but almost misses her step when her attention is distracted by his sudden movement. A nurse has joined him and he clasps her in a hug so that she looks over his shoulder and straight at Margaret. It is Noreen. Recognition is instant and mutual.

*

The living room into which Tony Ackers leads Harry is large and uncluttered. Like the tiny hall through which they've passed it is papered – or so the unobservant would allege – dove grey. Harry – beginning to practice a critical glance on everyone and everything he is about to leave – scrutinises the décor while Tony is checking whether anybody else is at home. His phrase. Harry decides the wallpaper was not originally grey and one coat of distemper only partly conceals a pattern of pagodas and weeping willows on Japanese bridges. Recalling Hopalong Bentham's critical approach – silently imitating his English master's tones, in fact – Harry deduces from the evidence that one coat of paint may point to poverty. Since this is not an aspect of the teaching profession he cares to linger on, he searches for another explanation. A hasty slapping with a wide brush might indicate that the occupants had no wish to put their tenancy on any permanent basis. Harry feels the place might be regarded as what the Forces refer to as a transit camp. Recalling the unworldliness of Vinnie, he constructs a third possibility. Tony and whoever it is with whom he shares may well have a take-us-as-you-find-us approach to visitors.

Somewhere, from beyond a closed door, he hears a slightly agitated conversation in progress and wonders whether he is welcome. This thought interrupts his examination of the sitting room only momentarily. The black carpet, though certainly not new, is something new to Harry. It stretches from white skirting-board to white skirting-board. It is the first house he has ever seen in which floor-boards are neither stained and covered with rugs or obscured by linoleum. He makes a mental note that a furnisher must be visited in South Wales to check the cost of wall-to-wall carpet in a study bed-sitting room.

There are bookshelves rather than bookcases. More accurately there are pine planks straight from a bomb site supported and separated from each other by a couple of bricks placed at intervals. Harry is about to implement the Hopalong Bentham test that one can gauge a man's mind by the books on his shelves when Tony reappears.

–Do you have to stand about looking spare, Harry? Coffee won't be long. I've managed to scramble up a few biscuits.

They face one another on two long sofas placed at right angles to the fire. The grate is cluttered with grey ash that cannot have been cleared for weeks since the early summer weather has been good.

–Why don't you brush that muck out, Tony? Fireplaces look quite attractive in the summer if you put a vase of flowers in them . . . or even some leaves from one of the parks.

Having spoken, he cannot think how he could have been crude enough to have commented on this, other than to realise his observation is based on a comparison with his parents' home.

Tony reacts with puzzled amusement so Harry attempts to soften his criticism with a smile. Since Tony doesn't drop his eyes Harry glances once more at powdered ash that almost obscures the acanthus pattern on tiles surrounding the grate.

–What a very constructive suggestion. Now why didn't either of us think of it, Tony? With subtle touches like that around the place we could be quite bold. Why not call in the photographers from *Homes and Gardens*? When they're demobbed. I see it now . . . a December evening . . . Tony and me either side of the fire like Darby and Joan . . . on second thoughts make that two china dogs. Presents from dear old Staffordshire. . .

Harry blushes, aware of aggressiveness underlying the irony of what is being said. The newcomer in the doorway is very much at home. Not only the coffee tray he carries but his waspish assurance indicate that. Harry prepares for a speedy retreat from any verbal battle he is certain he must lose.

–Harry, this is Eric. Eric, this is Harry who is going to be. . .

–A post-war interior designer of international renown. Am I right?

–No. I'm going to be a teacher. Like Tony. Do you teach as well?

–Reluctantly. Art . . . and a helping hand with History during the 'flu season. I have fading hopes of an escape from the classroom before chalk dust finally enters my soul.

Eric – or so Harry finds – is disturbing in some way not easily defined. His black curly hair is already speckled with a grey that matches the walls. There's a raw redness about his colouring and his skin would certainly be rough to the touch. Harry recoils from the pale blue glance that lingers on him and wonders again whether he has been wise in coming to the flat. It puzzles him that Tony, who is seemingly so civilised, should wish to share a roof with someone more full of muted anger than a caged animal. Not a man with whom one would wish to quarrel. The tongue would be savage and unpractised in forgiveness. Tony adds to Harry's discomfort by leaving the room to find a sugar spoon. Harry judges it best to sit silent or let Eric lead the conversation.

–So then . . . how does tomorrow's bright hope feel about the Sitwells?

–Do you mean what they read or the way that they read it?

–Rarer and rarer. You do have hidden talents, don't you? Quite the little fresh-cheeked critic. . . Hurry, Tony. Hurry. Your latest friend has high standards. Bring the Georgian fiddle back. There's no impressing Harry with anything but the best . . . just my little joke, chick, after a wearing week among the semi-morons. But we digress. What did impress you . . . the matter or the method, as they have it in the lecture rooms?

–It was a marvellous performance. I've never seen anything like it in the Town Hall. And they seemed to me – mind you, I'm only a suburban sixth-former – well, they seemed something from another world.

–I wouldn't quarrel with that. . .

–If you're implying that I'm ignorant, then you're right. But Tony's been on at me all the way here about other writers I should be studying. I've written down some of the names. I'm going to be a writer myself so I always carry a notebook, you see. Tony says it's high time somebody got to work on me.

–How right he is. You know Harry I don't think I need three guesses as to. . .

–Watch it, Eric. Harry isn't leaving sixth form for another few weeks.

–O, Harry doesn't have to worry about me, do you, chick? A north-country phrase in common usage. And I don't have to worry about his inexperience, do I?

–Well, I don't think so. I'm not exactly sure what you're driving at.

–Just ignore him, Harry, and have your coffee.

Little is said for a minute or so. Harry wishes Eric would leave. Tony wonders how he can ease Eric out without later repercussions. Eric enjoys his coffee in silence and smiles at first Tony and then at Harry. Tony goes across to the wind-up gramophone and puts on a record.

The melody is instantly recognisable to Harry. He finds it odd that the phrases should be performed by wind instruments rather than any of the sopranos he has listened to on the wireless. He looks forward to making an informed comment when the record ends. Tony listens to the music. Just once Eric smiles – a shade too sweetly – at the visitor.

Harry sits waiting while Tony turns over the record. Eric puts down his coffee cup and flicks a crumb from the front of his plain green shirt.

–Of course, you recognised it instantly, Harry?

Tony's interjection that recognition is less important than liking is not swift enough. Harry is eager to offer a relevant comment in this gathering of intellectuals.

–Well, of course. Mind you, I didn't know they'd done an orchestral version. It's the Anne Shelton song, isn't it? My voice has only just broken so I can only croak the words . . . they go *The sweetest song in the world is sung when lights are low and the heart is young.* . .

Eric runs his forefinger round the rim of the sugar bowl. He inspects the particles adhering to his skin and smiles. Tony puts down the record and closes the lid of the gramophone. Harry is conscious that something is amiss and wonders if he might have made what old Vinnie refers to as a fox's pass. He hopes Tony will – if necessary – come to his aid. It is Eric who speaks.

–The orchestral version, as you put it Harry, was first performed before Miss Shelton's young heart began to beat. You have just been listening to – charity being my middle name I shall not say hearing – the trio from the minuet in the thirty-ninth symphony by Wolfgang . . . Amadeus . . . Mozart.

–O . . . well . . . I shall know it when I hear it again.

–And perhaps you will fondly think of me. Until then I shall leave Tony to enlighten you on topics of mutual interest. Heed him, Harry. He will leave his mark on you as on a *tabula rasa*. The hour grows late and I must away to the wild woods where poor lost sailor boys stray in search of solace. In total war we must all give of our best, must we not?

With a trill of the wrist, that recalls for Harry the exit of some pantomime character, Eric leaves them. He also leaves the door ajar. Tony appears not to have noticed this yet Harry is sure he has done. The conversation which follows is pitched in a more intimate tone as though private to them both but with the understanding that, not too far away, every syllable is being savoured.

–You don't talk like a Londoner, Tony.

–You don't get many points for noticing that. I'm from Staffordshire. A provincial lad.

–That gives us something in common in a way. My father's people came from the edge of Exmoor. No one talks much about them. Except Grandmother Plimsoll and she lives out in Surrey now.

–Are you related to the M.P. of years ago?

–The Plimsoll Line you mean? Oh, yes. Let's see if I can get it right. His brother married my great-great-grandmother. I think that's it. Anyway they were farmers until they were sold up after the Napoleonic wars. So I'm a country boy a bit removed.

Tony – though Harry is scarcely aware of it – has crossed to a small table. Having poured a couple of glasses of Cyprus sherry he returns to the sofa. This time he sits next to his visitor.

–Why don't they all talk about that at home?

–Shouldn't think father would mind. I mean if I talked to him privately. If my mother were around it would give her another weapon to attack him. . .

–Attack him? You're joking?

–Only with words. She's riddled with silly snobbery. Spends half her time with her nose in a magazine reading about the private lives of dukes and such-like. . .

–They're not important to you?

–Why should they be? Like I told you about the Sitwells hardly touching me. I mean I'd rather hear something about a man like Sam Plimsoll. Not just because we're distantly related. . .

–Of course not. . .

–Not being funny at my expense, are you? Like Eric?

–Not at all, Harry.

–Well that's O.K. then. What I'm trying to say is that Samuel Plimsoll's a man who did some good. My grandmother took me along the Embankment when I was a kid and showed me his statue. The motto underneath referred to him as *The Sailor's Friend*. . .

There is a muffled explosion of giggles from somewhere not too far beyond the open door. Harry attributes this to an enthusiasm for a forebear that caused him to raise his voice. He hopes Tony will forgive this accidental outburst of family pride and looks sideways at his new friend. To Harry's surprise, Tony is blushing and this seems odd. He has never witnessed embarrassment in a qualified teacher. Eagerly he apologises for his gaffe.

–I'm sorry about that.

–No, Harry . . . I'm sorry. Eric has a warped sense of humour at times.

To underline his distaste for the intrusion on their conversation Tony closes the door.

–How did you meet Eric then? At college?

–Eh? Oh no. Works in the same school. He was there when I arrived. We come from more or less the same part of the world. Neither of us is married so . . . we share.

–How've you both managed to avoid the army?

–We're both excused boots. Me, literally. I've got flat feet, would you believe? Eric's got an eye defect. Good enough sight to teach Art but not so hot on the marksmanship.

–I think I'd like to share with another teacher when I've qualified. . .

–Who knows if I might still be around? I'm not quite coming up to retirement, yet.

–Exactly how old are you, Tony?

–Er, twenty-eight, if you must know. Must seem ancient. . .
–Not a bit. You'll hardly be thirty when I've done my
finals. And you don't act a bit old.
There is a silence which neither Harry nor Tony finds
disturbing. Harry's experience of being alone with
any male adult other than his father is slim. He enjoys
the moment and – with Tony beside him – has the sense
of something beginning. A friendship that offers more
potential than anything that can be expected of Paul
Harding.
–So? What're you thinking about, Harry?
–Thinking? Well, not a lot. Just how relaxed I feel . . .
being here.
–Shall I put some lights on?
–Please yourself. It's your home. I'm not worried. . .
–Fine. So . . . what now?
–Well, you could give me some more tips on what I should
be reading.
–Yes. Well, I suppose I could.
–You sound sort of disappointed. Have I said something
stupid again without realising it?
–No. Not at all, Harry. Not at all. I'll look out some novels
for you. And some of the books over there with orange
covers might not come amiss.
–Fine. I'll have a few weeks to myself soon. Anything you
can spare that might be useful. Damn. That word again.
Look, Tony. I can tell *you*. I want ideas. I've chucked out
all this churchy business which – as Harding says – leaves
a vacuum.
–Don't the family talk about anything? What the war's in
aid of, for instance?
–That's it. They don't. They see it as a kind of interruption.
Except my youngest uncle. He's away making a film. I'm
sure he's a socialist. In our family he keeps it to himself.
Don't think he trusts me yet.
–And you think I'm the one to come to for ideas?
–Well . . . as my grandmother would say . . . you must
have been around a bit.

–You like her?

–She's got none of the pretence all the rest seem to thrive on. Of course, if you don't trust me. . .

–Nonsense. Let's see what we can find. Come on over here. . .

As they stand side by side in front of the books there is more shadow than natural light in the room. Harry is impressed by Tony's ability to differentiate between the dozens of books by their shape and feel alone. To be sure that none of the limp cloth-covered volumes drops to the floor, Tony leans very close to Harry when placing them one by one in his ready hands. The fifth time that this happens he moves his head so near Harry's face that the light smell of brilliantine offers a scent more intoxicating than incense at High Mass. It could be the effect of the sunset or of the sherry or of the pleasure he finds in Tony's company that is about to prompt Harry to bury his nose in Tony's hair. With Harry a mere curl's breadth away from such a commitment, both men leap apart as the sirens begin to wail.

–Shit. . .

–. . . and derision as you would say. Are you scared of raids?

–Hardly. I'm a Messenger Boy.

–Then what?

–There'll be hell to play at home if they don't know where I am.

–They don't if you're on duty as a Messenger, do they?

–That's different, though I can't persuade them it's not logical.

–Your aunt won't have phoned?

–Daft old bat will be half-way down a gin bottle by now clutching her jewellery and her share certificates. I'll have to scoot for a bus. Quick.

–Look at your watch. It's gone eleven. . .

–Then I'll have to walk.

–Through a raid? That's madness. There's . . . we could make room for you here overnight. I mean you're welcome.

–That's very kind, Tony. I've a bed at home after all. Can't be more than half an hour from here. . .

–You're very welcome, you know.

–Maybe when I'm home from college.

–You might see things differently then. . .

–Not unless your books recommend Hitler's ideas I won't. . .

–I didn't mean that. Well, don't say I didn't warn you. . .

–Hold on. I'm nearly seventeen. . .

–And never been kissed?

Why should Tony demean himself with the wisecrack of what Margaret would call a red-nosed comedian Harry has still not worked out as he passes the ice rink on his way home. It had seemed such an awkward way to end the evening that his own lame reply

–Oh, I don't know about that–

had hardly jarred. He decides to relegate their final interchange to a mere footnote. The exciting discovery of Tony Ackers is likely to be of more enduring importance. He contemplates the likelihood of Tony remaining at the orphanage once the war is over and conscripted staff return to the classrooms. There's not a scrap of doubt that Tony has ability and intelligence and will therefore hold on to his job. Harry considers how possible it might be to ease Eric out of the flat. Although it must obviously have three bedrooms since overnight hospitality had been offered, life would hardly be tolerable with Eric's tongue constantly loosed on an unsophisticated newcomer. With sudden delight Harry realises that H. Plimsoll Dip. Ed. would no longer be a callow ignoramus against whom Eric could launch an offensive night and morning.

As he begins to stride through the deserted High Street the all-clear sounds. A window above the shoe repair shop opens before the sound fades and an old man calls out – not just to Harry

–False alarm. That's all we get now. The buggers are on the run.

★

101

When the last wave of bombers returning to Heston or Hanworth has passed, John Plimsoll concentrates again on the smaller sounds of the river: an occasional squawk of ducks in the reeds below the towpath; from time to time a cyclist passing behind him who calls *Good Morning*. John replies cheerily and wonders if this greeting, offered by strangers, signals a wish to demonstrate that everyone on the winning side should share in the good news from France. He is not optimistic that when the war is over such ease of contact will continue. In days when he was younger than Harry, neighbours smiled at one another in the markets and fellow dockyard workers waved across the Guildhall Square in Portsmouth. John accepts, with regret, that such a sense of community has passed and his post-war suburb is likely to revert to its pre-war bleakness.

He is careful not to turn his head when giving the time of day to these passers-by. Although it is a cloudless June morning, John wears his gabardine raincoat with the collar up. He has no wish to be recognised. Were he to be, only days would elapse before somebody would mention to one of the family that he – dependable as the church clock and more reliable than the trains – had not – between eight and eight-thirty precisely – been making for the station and a munitions factory. There would be endless questions concerning his health or his mental state. Perhaps not Vinnie and maybe not Harry would start probing. The rest would consider it odd to be sitting quite alone studying small craft bobbing on the Middlesex side of an island in the Thames.

John considers the explanation he might offer. He refuses to call it defence though he fears that is what it would be. He might say he had forgotten that a late start had been planned at the factory. A couple of shopping hours for everyone in celebration of monthly quotas exceeded and a congratulatory letter from the Ministry. This could hardly be contested and he could add nonchalantly that – having realised his mistake – the opportunity for a walk along the towpath while considering his future seemed too good to be missed. Having formulated his explanation, he readily sees that it could be used once only. His morning pattern – developed from the beginning of the year and the tiresome rows with Harry – would be disrupted. Unless he walked further afield. Beyond the railway bridge on the arterial road, perhaps, where the borough ended and Winifred's wretched Council friends would not bother to walk their snappy little dogs.

He fiddles in his pocket and selects a peppermint. Finding he has only two left in the bag, he makes a mental note to ask the tea lady if she can manage to fiddle another quarter of a pound off the ration at one of the corner shops along the Walworth Road. Margaret has never understood her husband's passion for peppermints and Vinnie has become too hazy about events at the turn of the century to recall why her son should prefer them to all other sweets. The Thames in 1944 might not be – John concedes – as tranquil and remote as Hayling Island in Victoria's Diamond Jubilee year but it is no tenth-rate substitute. John smiles at the recollection of himself as a ten-year-old on a celebratory picnic with china mugs all round and peppermints in a screw of paper for everyone. Each morning by the river he rehearses to himself that other summer when his world was undisturbed by intruders demanding decisions. Endless decisions. Income tax forms to be completed. Harry pestering for signatures on application forms for college or for a grant or a scholarship. Ministries making urgent demands on phones. Inspectors round every other day enquiring about vital components for tanks that should have been ready the day before yesterday. All exempt from the Forces and not one of them with the slightest inkling as to the practicalities involved.

With a sigh John extracts a last peppermint from its wrapping. He is not conscious of popping it into his mouth for his attention concentrates on extending his catalogue of woe to his home front. Even Vinnie irritates him as he visualises her slocking round each Sunday in broken shoes mutely hinting, in front of visitors, that he should do something about replacing a pair of old lace-ups that would disgrace a travelling gypsy. As for Margaret . . . John has for some years had a bet with himself on his homeward journey each Friday evening. Will the weekend be punctuated by suggestions that a dripping tap needs a new washer or will it be a tight-lipped Saturday until a garden fence is fixed so that Miss Griffith's cat can be restrained from messing all over the rockery?

Turning the splinters of his mint with care so the sweetness does not irritate a cavity in his molar, John feels almost inclined to warn Harry against settling to marriage and a mortgage. For a moment he feels keen to encourage his son's outlandish schemes for travelling around the globe with no fixed offer of work. If Harry's ideas seem against the natural order of things they can – John is prepared to allow – be no more than an extension of a mad world in which schoolboys fly planes and former medical students are prepared to participate in unspeakable experiments in concentration camps. Even the momentary contemplation of such vileness fills John with such revulsion that he concentrates his gaze on a trim cabin cruiser in which there's no sign of life. Perhaps at the weekends, when he himself has endless tasks about the house and on the vegetable plot, there are people all over the cruiser. A family, possibly, filling the cabin with laughter as good-natured as that which echoes back to John Plimsoll after forty years. Laughter from the yacht club at Hayling or the gardens of a pub crammed with apprentices.

From the inside pocket of his suit he pulls a battered black notebook. Other than an itemised list of loans to Harry for the purchase of ties and socks which no one but a questionable actor would wear, there are few entries. John unscrews his Parker pen and calculates just how much he would save privately if he gave up smoking. On the supposition that the war could not last more than another twelve months he calculates that he could celebrate peace in Europe by putting the deposit on a craft like the one gleaming in the sunlight no more than half a dozen breast strokes from the bench on which he sits. Vessels far less seaworthy had crossed to Dunkirk, though none had made enough speed to save Edmund. Come the first peacetime summer, a cabin cruiser would be ideal for nudging around the coast. Or – if the mines had not been cleared – then what better for adventuring up beyond Windsor and Maidenhead?

John pauses to consider what part his family might play in his project. He is appalled to realise he doesn't much care whether or not they would be interested. Not given to colourful expletives, John contents himself with damning and blasting Harry if river cruising is dismissed as banal. John does not suppose his own brother would be over-interested. Cliff appears to be further and further immersed in Council work and – once building supplies are available again – will be busier still with reconstruction work. John feels guilty that he does *not* feel guilty at having left Margaret until last. She could make up her own mind as to whether to share the weekends on the river or remain at home.

When he has counted the church clock striking nine John gets up. Any passing neighbour would be puzzled that he does not make for the station but for a bus stop that serves routes leading to the last villages of Middlesex. Heathrow and Sipson. There are no neighbours passing. If there were, John Plimsoll would be unlikely to tell them he is delighted to be going for an interview at a factory set in fields where – within weeks – the work force will be turning from tank spares to the production of bulldozers.

*

–Now look, Harry . . . when you turned up on the doorstep I told you I was getting ready to go on duty. . .
–Seemed the only way to be sure I was ever going to see you. Even when I can get the phone box at the corner to work, all I ever hear from your dad is that you're on duty

or helping your mother at the wool shop. Couldn't we at least walk down by the Baths and then cut up by the church to that bus stop? Noreen, it's not taking you out of your way and you could tell me what you think of the poem. . .

–I'm not really sure I want to. . .

–Want to what? Tell me about *Hands*?'

–Oh . . . that. . .

–What do you mean *that*?

Noreen sighs. She finds it tiresome that Harry has failed to understand the implication of her behaviour to him throughout July. As they stand at a corner by the queue outside the British Restaurant – to which neither of them gives any attention – she admits in fairness to herself that maybe she should have offered more honest explanations than a succession of extra duties and allusions to minor ailments. Her sigh is motivated both by this realisation and by an awareness that she resents an argument being forced upon her at a time and place not of her own choosing.

–Very well. Let's walk. The white lie I'll have to tell Sister will be on your conscience, Harry Plimsoll. Just pray she hasn't been watching to see if the buses are running on time today.

–Tell the old frump those doodlebugs after breakfast caused traffic delays and diversions. . .

Harry does not renew the question uppermost in his mind until they have reached the riverside. He waits until they have passed the very chestnut tree under which Miss Griffith alleges she surprised a man playing with himself.

–I'm not even sure how to say this. You'll only try to pick me up on the words I use. . .

–Try.

–Right. I don't even think it's just me that doesn't fit into your life. I'm not sure any girl would. Hold on. You asked me, so listen. All I hear from you nowadays is more and more about getting away from home and roaming off to the ends of the earth. There's no mention of settling and – to tell you the truth – I don't much relish sleeping with my head on a haversack and making do with an ordnance survey map for a bedcover.

–Noreen, that's great. That's a wonderful way of putting it. Can I use it in my next poem?

–Christ Almighty, Harry Plimsoll. There you go again. I don't want my hands in a ruddy old poem, or my bra, or my life. That's telling you. And another thing I've been meaning to tell you for weeks . . . always supposing that gracious mother of yours hasn't dropped a not so subtle hint. . .

–What's all this, then? Now what are you on about?

–You'd better know that I've been seeing someone else.

To Harry, this information is somewhat more astounding than, say, the unexpected occurrence of a bomb crater beneath his feet. He has no opportunity to think over how far he may have presumed on Noreen or regarded her as a necessary appendage to a clean-shaven and apparently respectable adolescent. He is quite winded by this reference to a rival and replies stiffly without looking at Noreen.

–Well . . . if that's how it is . . . there's nothing more to be said. Unless of course you're making it up to get me jealous.

–Don't be so damned dramatic. I didn't say I was engaged to him. He's a Canadian. Your mother saw me with him . . . a few weeks back. She's probably storing that up like a secret weapon. . .

–And, of course, the Canadian Mountie has got lots of dollars. Theatres and dances and sweets off the ration and nylons, no doubt. . .

–Well, I had to risk hurting your pride. More to the point, Clark has some consideration for me. He makes me feel a person . . . not just something sitting around waiting until it occurs to him to call.

–So we're finished, then?

–Harry, do you have to sound like a B-feature film? All I'm saying is, I'm bored with listening to you wanting to tear off and rearrange the world. . .

–You don't think it needs it?

–I do spend my time looking after undernourished kids. Credit me with something.

–Well, there's something we can build on. . .

–No, Harry. It's more than that with you. I just have this feeling you like all the upheaval of the war. You'll resent peacetime. There'll be no settling down for you. . .

–Not here there won't be.

–Or anywhere, I suspect. Come on. Walk me to the bus or there'll be snide remarks about arriving early for night shift when I sign in.

Harry walks in silence. He realises his apprehension is little more than selfishness. It is too late in the year to leave Noreen to her Canadian and seek out another girlfriend whose studio portrait could stand on his desk at college and whose letters would arrive with gratifying punctuality each Tuesday morning. He decides to go for a compromise.

–You're not thinking of marrying this what's his name? Clark?

–No, I am not. And I'm not thinking of marrying you or anyone else at the moment. Are you sure you're really the marrying kind?

This is something Harry has never formulated for himself. To have thought of himself as free from the encumbrances he has noted in his family and neighbours has long been axiomatic to him. Has been a matter for exultation. Noreen's words convey to him something disturbingly close to social censure. For no accountable reason other than that they are the only bachelors he knows, he thinks of Tony and Eric. He wonders whether all bachelors, as they glide through their twenties, acquire the waspish oddities of Eric. This unwelcome possibility is quickly obliterated by the image of Tony. Warm and companionable and understanding Tony.

–And what's that supposed to mean?

–Whatever you want it to. Not even so sure myself. It's a phrase Sister used to describe one of our doctors. Anyway, I'd say it fits you in your present mood. Maybe you'll change. We all will, I expect.

–I suppose this means you won't write to me at college?
–Honestly. You're like one of our kids having a tantrum.
Yes, I'll write. It'll be something to do on night duty
when the little ones have stopped coughing or wetting
themselves. . .
–And I'll be as good a way of passing the time as any?
–Think of what you've just said, Harry Plimsoll. Maybe
that's how you've thought about me. Don't be so damn
self-pitying. Christ . . . there's my bus. Do I still get
invited to your birthday party. . . ?
–As long as you don't drag the Mountie with you. . .
–You'll have to keep guessing, won't you?

★

The first explanation that occurs to Harry is the possibility
of a puncture. Despite the care that Joe lavishes on his
three-speed Raleigh, a puncture has to be a possibility.
Refusing to consider the consequences, Harry thrusts
his own flashlamp into his greatcoat pocket. It is no
longer important to him to preserve the shape and cut
of this garment. Within hours it will be returned to the
clothing depot. Very probably never reissued. Stooping
to tug off his cycle clips, he improvises further reasons
for the Raleigh not being in its usual place at the end of
the rack. There might have been a recurrence of Joe's
mother's bronchitis. A damp end to the summer would
certainly account for that and it would follow that Joe
himself would have been delayed through having to cook
the evening meal. Only as Harry trudges towards the
dim light above the oak doors does he allow himself
to speculate that Joe might have been involved in an
accident. In admitting this, he is torn between a concern
for Joe and a very personal frustration that their last shared
night duty will not develop as he has planned it – in
exciting detail – for the past three evenings.
With his back to the doors, Harry lingers on the off-
chance that he will catch Joe whistling his way through the
bushes as his racer grinds along the gravel paths. He

wonders what the reaction would be if – say around midnight – it were suggested that they write to each other. Not too regularly. Not the weekly letter to Noreen. And, of course, there'd be no question of exchanging photographs. But a letter, perhaps once a fortnight, would surely not be thought odd by Joe's parents. Everybody knew that soldiers wrote to their mates. Schoolchildren everywhere were regularly encouraged to write to lonely service men and women in the Far East and in prisoner of war camps.

The drizzle is beginning to thicken to a steady downpour as Harry turns to open the doors. If Joe is not turning up then the night duty will have to be shared with some boring stranger. Whoever that may be, Harry himself is determined to make for whichever part of the borough they're assigned via a quick call at Railway Cottages. It's no part of his calculation that Joe's parents might be embarrassed by the arrival of a scrubbed and brylcreemed youth who has used an after-shave lotion for the very first time.

He pushes aside the double set of blackout curtains and blinks in the glare of the reception area. Charlie is at his usual table working on elaborate rosters. Harry sniffs once and relaxes. None of the Messengers other than Joe smokes Woodbines. He is waiting, perhaps, around a corner among the fold-away chairs and thumbing through a dog-eared copy of Lilliput. Harry does not glance too searchingly, having long since discovered that Senior Messenger Charlie is more than just a dab hand with rosters and shift patterns. Joe agrees there is something canine about Charlie's face. He also agrees with Harry that canine Charlie is also an expert at sniffing dirt. Charlie makes no secret of his own assumption that sex is everybody's underlying preoccupation. Harry feels that Charlie's stories of his own upbringing near the Tower must account for this. To have been giving lonely bachelors a quick wank down dark alleys by the docks while still at Junior School seems astounding but Joe contends it's factual.

110

Charlie glances for a second as Harry approaches the table. He does not look up again until he has finished pencilling in a couple of names.

–Made it at last, eh, Plimsoll? Honest . . . you'll be late coming on your own honeymoon.

When their eyes meet Harry is sure Charlie knows and is concealing something. It can be nothing that concerns Noreen. Harry has been careful to establish that she exists and to stress that she's something more than a handful of tit after the last waltz. How much of this Charlie has believed, Harry neither knows nor cares.

–Very droll, Charlie. Fact is I had to clear out this case. Brought my civvies in it for the morning.

–Fair enough. I'll check your things with you before you go off duty.

–So . . . where's it to be tonight, Charlie?

From somewhere behind and to his left a renewed scent of Woodbine drifts towards Harry. He interprets this fancifully as a smoke signal from Joe that all will be well. Charlie meditates a moment and chews the end of his pencil. He sniffs before answering and Harry becomes wary. The hound is on the hunt.

–Had you down to go over past the sewage farm with Smedges. . .

The combination of the borough's least desirable outpost and Smedges is too much. One such experience months back had been more than sufficient. Harry explodes without caring whether Smedges may be in earshot.

–You're bloody joking. He farts all night. Smedges stuffs his face with pies and chips at the canteen and stinks the room out worse than the shit farm next door. Surely, Charlie, on my last night I can have some. . .

–If you wanted to be choosy you should have gone for my job, mate. The rules are the rules but seeing as it is your last duty we'll bend them a bit. Who would you like to go with?

–Well . . . anyone but Hedges for a start.

The conversation is becoming public and Harry hopes he has lowered his voice sufficiently to avoid his seeming indifference being hurtful to Joe. Charlie makes some play with his index finger. He runs it up and down the roster sheet with accompanying sighs and clucks. Abruptly he drops the roster sheet and picks up a scrap of paper. Since he holds it away from Harry only Charlie can know if anything – or nothing – is scribbled on it.

–Nearly forgot. We sorted out this little problem before you ambled in. If you'd been here on the dot, Plimsoll, there wouldn't have been no bother. Joe Gibbs asked specially if you could be together. Nice to have a considerate mate, eh?

Harry swallows and stares at the table. Charlie – he is convinced – is about to lob a tiny anti-personnel device at him.

–Well . . . thanks for letting me know, Charlie. I mean I get on well enough with Gibbs. . .

–You take the words out of my mouth, Harry. I've sat here for weeks now thinking how nice to see two decent young blokes cycling away to help the war effort and natter about their girlfriends. . .

–So what's wrong with that? What are you hinting?

–Hinting? Me? Nothing. Nothing at all. What should I be hinting?

–Well implying or insinuating or some bloody thing. . .

Harry intends to end the skirmish there. Yet – as so often in his short past – once in an argument he has offered too much and now regrets it. In this instance there is a difference. He is aware of what he is doing as he shapes the words that ensnare him. There is even a milli-second for him to resolve that in future – maybe in college debates – he will remain as cool as a pilot cornered in a dog-fight.

–What's eating you, Harry? You know me. If I'm going to say anything then I come straight out with it. Anyone'd think I was suggesting you and Gibbs are having a bit on the side. Course, I was dragged up among blokes who liked a bit of the other. You'd be amazed. Even boxers and real hard villains. But not here, Harry boy. Least of all with you. I mean we all know you're off to be a respectable member of the middle classes. What else could you be but a good influence on Joe Gibbs, eh?

–O.K. Let's leave it, shall we?

–Sure. I've got things to sort out even if you haven't. Gibbs is back there waiting for you. Who knows . . . might have a goodbye present he'll slip you later.

There's little doubt in Harry's mind that Charlie knows what has happened for many weeks and what will happen in the privacy of a locked room within an hour. No one has ever expressed a wish to stay at Headquarters with Charlie. Harry wonders whether there might not be some envy in Charlie. Reassured that everything will be well on his last duty, Harry relaxes and turns the chit-chat to Charlie's own existence beyond the temporary joys of being a boss.

–So how's it going, then? I mean working here during the day?

–Can't complain, Harry.

–That'd be a change.

–Well. Let's face it. Who can say what's on the cards when this lot's over? I'm not too struck with the prospect of ex-service heroes bunging up the corridors, that's for sure. Where's me chances of promotion in the Planning Office then? What's more, there'll be me call-up papers arriving with Santa Claus this year. Tell you what, though, Plimsoll. I'm going to have bladder trouble or a touch of the kidneys. No square-bashing for Charlie. . .

–But there's nothing wrong with. . .

–You always were bloody simple, Harry. How long did it take you to catch on that your best mate – your former best mate – Harding was having it off with that Naylor bird from the convent?

–I was talking about your kidneys.

–So you were. Well I'm working on it, see? Couple of months back I started slipping a dozen eggs a week to Doctor Dawkinson for his kids' tea. Now if I had to become a latrine wallah, he'd miss all that, wouldn't he?

–One flaw in your logic, Charlie. Once the war's over he won't need your eggs.

113

–There you go again. Simple Plimsoll. You wouldn't feel people pissing all over you. Listen. Just because they start lighting sparklers in Trafalgar Square it don't follow in logic, or any other sodding thing, that we'll all be stuffing ourselves with peaches and cream the next afternoon, does it?

–You may be right.

–You can bet your virginity on that. Always supposing you haven't lost it already. Speaking of which you'd better collect Joe and bugger off to Craneside. Just think of me slaving here on me rosters and wondering who does what to which. . .

–Give it a rest will you, Charlie?

–Let's hope you two do before dawn. Cheers, Harry boy.

–See you about eight.

Joe is not thumbing through Lilliput. His back rests on a pillow he has up-ended against the wall and his legs dangle from the lowest of a tier of bunks. His legs are much straighter than the blue serge trousers that cover them. A pair of thin grey summer socks patterned with maroon lozenges hang limply over his shoes. He welcomes Harry with a wink and eases himself to his feet.

Joe's trousers hang from his waist like twin concertinas. Harry recalls his mother's observation that uniforms can do wonders for the most ungainly. Looking at Joe, he becomes aware that such an observation begs the question that the wearer wishes to do something with the uniform. Joe does not. Very obviously it has never occurred to him to ask his mother or his girlfriend to tailor the waistband of his tunic or take a tuck in the seat of the trousers. Harry tries to equate Joe's present sloppiness with the neatness of his appearance on afternoons when they have cycled off along the towpaths. He can only conclude that Joe is saying, implicitly, that the Messenger work is something to be got on with like the rest of the war. As they move from the rest area, Harry does wonder why Joe ever bothered to volunteer for the job. He guesses – it can be no more – that maybe Civil Defence provides a twice a week escape from Railway

Cottages. From endless parental bickering or an equally overpowering routine of Garrison Theatre and variety shows on the wireless.

–Thought you'd never finish nattering on with Charlie. How's it been going then?

–Fine. Now. Thought you weren't going to turn up.

–Just thought I'd get you worried. You were worried, weren't you?

–Was I?

–Bloody liar. You were. Bet you searched for the bike. Bet you.

They are nearing the door and Harry is sure of two things. One – Charlie is listening, which wouldn't be difficult since Joe is speaking as openly as he would when suggesting a game of darts. Two – Harry himself is blushing. Careful to look only at the blackout curtains as he drags the first set aside, he replies with a nonchalance that hardly deceives himself let alone Joe or Charlie.

–So, where is it? Had a prang? Do I have to give you a lift?

–Hid it in the laurel bushes to have you on, didn't I?

–You stupid bugger. Could have had your lamp nicked by someone from the Youth Club or one of the choirboys on his way home. They go for lamps. Pumps too.

Joe extracts his cycle lamp from the wrinkled depths of his tunic and the pump from his left sleeve.

–Wasn't born yesterday, Harry. Come on, will you? It's going to take us more than half an hour to get ourselves over to Craneside. Be gone ten before we get sorted out. Won't leave much time for talking or anything. . .

Harry repeats to himself Joe's last words and is fairly sure how he should interpret them. He anticipates being very close in the shadows cast by a watery moon playing through such leaves as still remain on the chestnut trees in the Craneside school yard. Being naked yet still warm even with the bottoms of the long casement windows pushed up. Being relaxed in a way that had not seemed possible until a casual wrestling dispute had led to a clinch in which undreamed-of landscapes became illuminated through mutual delight.

–You're right, Joe. We must talk. There's a lot I've got to say. . .

–I know better than to try stopping you, chum.Not too many long words though, eh? Don't go thinking I haven't noticed you sounding more and more like a dictionary since you started reading up all those books for college.

–Promise I won't. Is it too late to get some chips?

–Shouldn't think so. Look . . . lights are still on. Want salt and vinegar. . . ?

–I'll get them.

–You'll shut up and mind me bike. I'm buying.

★

The silence is punctuated only by Joe's long inhalation and exhalation of cigarette smoke. In that silence Harry wonders whether Joe – having stubbed the end – might pull up the blankets and grunt *Goodnight*. It is not a memory Harry would wish to carry with him to South Wales. He is determined that Joe shall not recede in the coming weeks to the sweet scent of Woodbines intermingled with a mop of sketchily combed ginger hair. Even a more private recollection of that same hair against his lips as Joe mutters *that feels good Harry*, will not suffice. Nor does he intend to content himself at college merely with the conscious effort of conjuring up the feel of Joe's calloused hand on his own less pimply shoulder at the moment of climax.

Yet if there is to be anything more enduring between them than one summer's outings and a dozen shared nights – and Harry feels strongly that there should be – he knows he himself must initiate it. He needs to know what Joe is thinking. Silences remind Harry uncomfortably of home.

He turns his head so that he can look more easily at Joe and begin a discussion. As he does so, Joe – supposing that Harry's neck is cramped – also shifts a little. Harry's own head drops forward and he looks for the first time at Joe's uncircumcised cock resting in

116

the shadow of a thickly furred thigh. Moonlight catches a last bead of sperm not wiped from it. Harry gulps at his own bewildering urge. Only the thought of shocking Joe deters him from leaning to lift it away with the curled tip of his tongue. Joe yawns in a contented way and Harry casts wildly around for any commonplace that will distract Joe's attention – and his own – from the stirring in his crotch.

–D'you think it's midnight yet?

–Who cares, eh? Feeling shagged already, Harry boy?

Catching each other's glance they giggle at the overtones of the verb.

–Course not. You?

–Don't fret about me. I don't have to give myself brain fatigue with piles of deep books.

–And I don't have to face a ten-hour day delivering groceries.

–You make it sound like digging in the bloody mines. I'm as fresh as a daisy.

–Good. Then we can talk.

–If we have to. Hang on, though. Got a treat for you.

Joe hops deftly across the stretchers, careful not to unbalance them. Although rainclouds have begun to obscure the moon, Harry can still watch Joe's slightly heavy thighs and calves as he stumps away to their topcoats hanging behind the classroom door. He tries to imagine how Joe might look even in two years. If he continues cycling as a hobby he'll remain trim. Once married to Elsie who might – or might not – be a resourceful cook, Joe could easily put on weight. Harry experiences a surge of irritation at the thought of Joe married to Elsie. Not a jealousy of Elsie. Not even annoyance at the likelihood of Joe or himself or Harding or Charlie or anyone marrying. Before Joe is back and kneeling naked by him, Harry has barely time to define his irritation as being an impatience with Joe himself for the uncomplaining acceptance of settling down and forgetting all the green April mornings that could be.

117

They sit with shoulders touching, drinking the bottle of cooking sherry which – both agree – tastes like sticky peppered water.

–Joe?

–Mmmm?

–Have you ever done . . . what we've been doing these past months . . . with a girl? With Elsie, say?

Joe scoops a hand behind him round the parquet floor until he finds his cigarettes. There are two left. Once again he offers the packet to Harry who shakes his head.

–Go on. I've got another ten.

–Thanks. No. Well . . . have you?

–Wouldn't have it, would she? Not saying she doesn't let me have a feel around. Up top mainly. Enough to get me going, anyway. Well, it would get anyone going, wouldn't it? Then she expects me to carry on strolling with sore balls.

–And that's it?

–Well . . . couple of times I've tried to get her to do what you do for me. Not sure she'd be as considerate as you, though. She'd make it more of a favour like. Anyway, it's not on so far as Elsie's concerned. Catholic, see? Wait till the wedding bells and all that. How 'bout you then?

Harry enumerates to himself experiments not merely with Noreen. One or two of the convent fifth-formers after joint dancing classes on Friday afternoons. Earlier too. Behind the statues in the Town Hall gardens before Saturday-morning cinema with Katie from Junior School. Before Katie and her brother left for Canada at the beginning of the war with a shipload of children who never arrived.

–Not really. Well, not all the way like.

Fortified with a second half-teacup of cooking sherry, Harry is ready to ask his second – equally urgent – question.

–How about with any other bloke then, Joe? Did it ever happen before we did it?

–Never. Wasn't even sure, when we were larking around, what was happening.

–But you didn't feel shocked?

118

–Whatever for? Don't tell me you don't enjoy it. . .

–You'd know I was lying even if you didn't say so.

–Man of few words, mate. What about you, though? With other fellows?

Embarrassment is like a flame scorching the back of Harry's neck. He wills himself not to remember Harding lying so close on the sand. Was the noisiness of his breathing the result of their swim or of anticipation? For eighteen months, Harry has no more been able to resolve this than whether Harding's eyes were screwed against the sunlight or were really smiling.

–No. Never.

–There we are, then. Two more lads who lost their virginities in the turmoil of war, eh? Hey . . . you reckon this does count, Harry? Doing it with a bloke does mean you've lost your cherry?

–Suppose so. Whatever it means I'm glad it's been with you.

–You say some daft things.

–I meant that. It was you mentioned the war. We'd never have met . . . I mean. . .

–What you mean is, college boys wouldn't dream they'd anything in common with delivery boys unless the war'd shoved 'em up against one another.

–Not like us though. With no clothes on.

–Wouldn't amaze me. Bloke next door to us was on leave from the R.A.F. back in . . . May, it'd be. Told us a whole camp in North Africa had to be broken up. All the local tarts was poxed to the eyebrows so the Padre tipped the lads the wink and they all got on with it. Can't blame 'em. That desert heat must make anyone sexy.

Harry follows this anecdote with a grunt. Even while Joe has been speaking, Harry is more concerned with his own sense of completeness in the company of his friend. A feeling of being at home more forceful than any he has ever experienced in his parents' house. It surpasses even that delight he has known since childhood whenever he has stayed with old Vinnie.

–Where've you been?

–Been?

–Well, you don't look tired and you don't sound drunk so you must have spent the last minute at that college of yours already.

–Not really.

–Soon will be, though. Can't reckon on seeing much of you after that, can I?

–Why not? We could meet at Christmas for a drink. . .

–Would it be the same though, Harry boy?

As he asks this, Joe up-ends the sherry bottle against Harry's mouth. The dregs must either trickle down his throat or onto his throat and chest. He opens his mouth and Joe slides the rim of the bottle gently until it rests on the very back of Harry's tongue. Joe raises one eyebrow in the way he invariably does when suggesting they might both head their bikes to some unexplored turning rather than return immediately by a usual route. Harry senses the colour rising from his neck to his cheeks and covers this with a splutter so that Joe has to remove the bottle and turn away.

–See what I mean, Harry? Not much chance of us carrying on like this in the middle of the Waterman's, eh?

Having set the empty bottle rolling along the parquet floor, Joe flops back and rests his head across Harry's thighs. Not for the first time in Joe's company, Harry knows what his friend wants to happen without any words or carefully shaped questions. He attempts to tighten his thighs beneath Joe's head so that it will not be obvious how strongly the prospect excites him. As an extra safeguard he begins to chatter.

–Anyway, you'll be getting a holiday next year, won't you? Why not take the week off after Easter? That would give us ten days. Or in the summer – one side or other of the August bank holiday. We've got the bikes. I could borrow my cousin's tent. . .

–He might want it.

–Poor sod got blown to bits at Dunkirk.

–Not much use to him then, is it? Good bloke, was he?

As Joe's words penetrate and Harry evaluates them, he thinks of picnics with cousin Edmund. Thirteen-year-old Edmund with a whiff of sweat already under the arms of a cream summer shirt. There *had* been an afternoon before Harding smiled up from the sand. Edmund's hazel eyes assessing his younger cousin and never glancing away.

–A good bloke. Who knows? He might have been a better one, too. . .

–Right. Now, say for argument's sake you're still of a mind to go tazzing off on the bikes next year. . .

–I proposed it, didn't I?

–Fair enough. And say again I haven't had me call-up papers, Harry. Where'd you reckon we should go?

–The Lake District?

–The how much? You don't catch me going up there. Too bloody nippy on the old balls, mate. Mum's got a sister lives Preston way. White their faces are when they come for a holiday. White just like suet duff with a couple of raisins for peepers. We'll go west, Harry boy.

–Suits me. That's where my dad's family came from.

–I'm not hunting round no gravestones. You can forget that.

–Who even suggested it? Do we agree on Devon?

–Mum and Dad went there for their honeymoon. The landlady rushed 'em so much Mum had to take cheese and jam sandwiches enough to last three days. . .

–What did they eat for the rest of the fortnight?

–Fortnight? You should be doing a comic turn on the wireless, you should. They could only scrape up enough for the August weekend. We could do better'n that though, if we put a bit aside until Easter, eh? Yeah. Devon sounds good.

Joe indicates that for him the discussion is over by lifting his head a moment. He rests it again almost as it had been across Harry's thighs, except that his arms are now folded under his neck, serving as a pillow. Very lightly his finger tips begin to weave through Harry's pubic hair. The reaction is immediate and Harry is glad Joe cannot see how his open mouth is taut with excitement and his fingers claw at the canvas of the stretcher. He is even unaware that Joe has paused and has swivelled in one movement so that their faces are a breath apart. Joe has to whisper a second time before Harry is conscious that he has been asked a question.

–What?

–I said . . . would you hate me if I kissed you?

–I don't seem to be doing very much to stop you, do I?

Neither closes his eyes. Harry finds Joe's lips exciting. Less yielding than Noreen's. In Joe's kisses there is a firmness. An unpredictability, too, that hints less at a quest for oblivion than a sudden breakaway and an alternative expression of affection in some verbal – even physical – clinch. Harry raises his taut fingers from the stretcher frame to place them on Joe's cheek-bones. Holding his friend's face steady, he raises his own head to return the kiss. At their second contact Joe's lips open and their tongues begin a tentative discussion.

It is Joe who pulls back from Harry's grip. His mouth still slightly open and his thighs parting on either side of Harry's he edges down so that his lips – damp from their kisses and sticky with the sherry – glide between the straining muscles of Harry's chest. Joe's lips cover Harry's navel and his tongue-tip loiters there, circling the surround of softer flesh. Harry's fingertips clamp round Joe's shoulders more obsessively than they had held the metallic stretcher frame moments before. His words break from his constricted throat in an ecstasy.

–Wait. Joe. . . Hold it. Joe . . . don't make me come yet.

So Joe lifts his head. He too waits, anticipating that Harry will flick round with the agility of a dolphin. They exchange no words or looks or gestures as their mouths dive to taste the sweetness that their hands already cup.

*

–There's just no pleasing any of you today. Young Harry carried on at me all the way to Waterloo. . .

–What was he moaning about?

Vinnie removes her darned summer gloves before answering. Having smoothed them, she places them at the bottom of her shopping bag on the empty chair. Beyond the scrubbed deal tables she surveys a queue that quite obscures the counter.

–When do we get this skate? Didn't tell me he'd gone to Margate to catch the damned thing.

–Hang on, will you? Best fish and chips south of the river they serve here. He's back there cooking it fresh and crispy for you. And don't try evading the issue with me, Vinnie Cosser. Even as a toddler you was keen to turn the subject when you'd pooped yer drawers. So . . . what's wrong with young Harry?

–Nothing's wrong with him. Why should there be? What I meant wasn't so much anything he said. The way he looked. The Plimsolls all gather their lips to a miser's purse when they're disapproving. . .

–Still haven't told me. Stop wittering. . .

–He didn't like the way his grandmother was dressed to come out for the day. I told him – just as I've told you – I'm off on a bit of bargain hunting. How far would I get in Winifred's fur coat, I'd like to know? Or one of Margaret's fancy hats?

Walter Cosser watches his sister pick up first their knives and then the forks from the table. She breathes on each and cleans it with the hem of her apron. Had she been anyone other than his sister he would have dismissed this as middle-class snootiness and asked whether the surroundings weren't classy enough. Vinnie's gesture carries him back almost seventy years to their own grandmother's fanaticism for cleanliness. A house saturated with the smell of soap and disinfectant as though endless scouring and rinsing could bring back a husband killed in the last outbreak of cholera.

When Vinnie looks up Walter is smiling.

–Wasn't just to please me, then, you came out in your gardening frock? Come on, Vinnie. Let's have the truth. Wouldn't you rather be having a bite with your fine friends at the Ritz?

–Don't be foolish, Wallie. I've never been in the Ritz in my life. I like nice things. Who in their right mind doesn't? So far as fine friends go, I don't have any. No. You listen. Alice used to say I should have been an actress. Maybe she wasn't far wrong at that. I might act up to Winifred's awful councillors if there's a nip of sherry on the go or a garden party. Doesn't stop me having a private laugh at it all. What'd you expect me to do? Sit at home on a pension and learn to chat to myself?

–You could come and see me more often.

–Maybe I will. Ah . . . here's the skate. That wing'll do for me. Give it here.

–Have you got a couple of glasses, mate? Me rich sister's treating us to a bottle of stout. Bring three and I'll pour a drop for you. Must be thirsty work.

Brother and sister peel back the crisped batter of the fish before flaking aside the sweet, white flesh with their knives. As Walter does so he resolves not to twit Vinnie further. He had planned to ask if she'd suggested a fish and chip lunch as a bit of slumming to put him at his ease. Overriding this is his curiosity about the family with whom he has so little contact. He swallows a mouthful of stout.

–So what makes your journey really necessary, Vinnie? Come to persuade me to starch a collar and drop over for Christmas, have you? Want me to sit while Winifred shrieks her way through *The Lost Chord* again? That it, eh? Let bygones be bygones?

Vinnie picks up the perforated aluminium salt pot. In her compact hand it looks larger than a half-pint measure. She scatters salt into her palm and dusts it over her plate. Glancing quickly to ensure she isn't being observed, she picks up a couple of chips with her fingers and nibbles them as she replies.

–Yes and no to that, Wallie. I don't expect you for Christmas. Truth to tell, I sometimes wonder how many more Christmases the Plimsolls will have together. However that may be . . . doesn't alter facts. It has to be bygones for both of us Wallie, old stick, doesn't it?

Having wiped his moustache with the back of his hand, Walter chews slowly until his mouth empties. He does not drop his eyes from his sister whose bright glance daunts him. Before putting the question he hesitates to ask, he runs his tongue round the stump of a tooth that no longer troubles him.

–Not trying to tell me you're on your way to the bone yard, are yer, gel? No bad news from the quack, is it?

–You always were a soft ha'p'th under all that hard-boiled politics, Wallie Cosser. Wouldn't do you much good if we had your blooming old revolution, would it? There's nothing wrong with me so don't stare as if you're measuring me up for my box already. Days like this I don't feel a minute over forty. If you want the truth . . . well . . . I just had this feeling a couple of days back when I arranged to come up with Harry. Not that he knows where I am.

–Where's he?

–Buying college books.

–And what's this feeling then? There's more in this, Vinnie, than you're letting on. I'm not straight off the boats, yer know. . .

Vinnie twists her wedding ring. Walter doesn't comment but he guesses she is recalling her married life. Perhaps contrasting that with her old age and no one but herself to cook and care for.

–Put it this way, Wallie. We've both had our three-score years and ten. If it should please the good Lord to take me one of these. . .

–Marx Almighty. What you on about, woman? We'll have you up here all through Victory night doing the hokey cokey round Nelson's column with the rest. Eat yer chips. No one's measuring you up yet.

–Maybe you're right. Perhaps it's because I'm alone more now. I've got my garden and the pickling and the wine-making. Yes, I've plenty of books I can reread and a wireless, too, that Cliff gave me. But I'm still alone long enough to get what's called a presentiment. Know what that is?

125

–Oh, I know all right. The rent collector's step on the stairs two minutes before you really hear it.

–Yes. And didn't I come up to tell you Edmund had gone long before we had any telegram and the papers started calling it the miracle of Dunkirk?

–Alright. So it's not all in the textbooks. No call for you to start worrying everyone silly though. Got me all of a tremble. . .

–Well, you can't say I didn't raise the subject. And I'll tell you for why – how about filling my glass while you're at it? – as well. If anything should happen to me – no, just say it should – you're to keep an eye on Harry.

–Going off the rails, is he?

–What a thing to say. . .

–Use yer common, gel. I'm out of touch with all the lot of you. I wouldn't even know where to find the kid.

Vinnie blows her nose and takes a sip of stout. She appears to be picking over the last of her chips to establish whether there is anything other than shrivelled ends.

–And you're not going to. Unless it's necessary. He's off to college and that's sufficient.

–Yes, yes, yes. Jack told me that much when he breezed in months ago. So what's the problem? Booze? Too fond of the skirts, is he? Or is it. . .

–Nothing like that. Wallie . . . there's a bit of you in Harry. Wanting to put the world to rights with politics. That doesn't worry me. . .

–Bloody delights me, I can tell you. Someone to carry on the struggle. . .

–I'll have to struggle to keep me patience unless you get the rest of that down you and listen. It's that mother of his. . .

–Comes of a bullying lot. Ought to turn it on the profiteers not on each other. . .

–May I finish? I'd have said the McCawdies are profiteers living on their family's feelings. Never mind. Our John's never been able to stand up to her. . .

–Once I told her she should have married one of her own brothers, not him. . .

126

–No one's asking for your disgusting suggestions. John would have her with that silent suffering Madonna look of hers she puts on.

–Who sent him off to church as a nipper, then? We all fall for what we see around us. . .

–That's why young Harry's not tearing up here to meet your friend Red Ellen Wilkinson. He's not spending the rest of his life organising hunger marches, so just rest assured of that.

–No more hunger when this lot's over, Vinnie.

–You've been sitting there idling with that pipe of yours for I don't know how long. Light the darned thing and listen while I finish. . . Now. Harry needs kindness. Starved of it in that mausoleum of a house, he is. The lust can look after itself. He won't go back there when he's finished this college course of his. Don't go imagining he'll be moving into the Buildings with you. Wouldn't be right for a schoolmaster to have to mangle his shirts on a public landing and trail down I don't know how many flights to empty his slops in the snow. All I'm guessing is that young Harry will find himself someone sooner than most. It won't be some silly little mouse from the next street, either. He isn't all our side of the family, Wallie. Underneath he's as tough as that mother of his, whether he knows it or not. She suspects it. That's why they spit like cat and dog all the time. When he does make his choice – and I may not be here to see it – you just mind you tell him you're sure he's doing the right thing. Whatever you think, you support him. There. I've had my say. Trust you to finish the last of the stout. After that, I could do with something to wet my whistle.

–So what if he shows up on me doorstep with a geisha girl? Or a six foot Cossack?

–It'll be his choice. I've had my life and you've had yours. I'm off to powder my nose and then I must think about a train.

When Vinnie pushes back past the queue of customers, she finds Wallie has already paid the bill. Her brother is standing in the street with his back to the shop window.

On the pretence of fiddling with the button of her glove she watches as he blows his nose repeatedly. Above the noise of the fish frying and the till, she can hear him through the open doorway noisily clearing his throat.
–Soft ha'p'th.

*

Gently – so that the spine should not be damaged – Harry rests his book face down on the tablecloth. He wraps a clean handkerchief around the metallic handle of the hot water jug and refills his pot of tea for one. He rather hopes the second cup will be less strong and harsh to the taste than the first. On the evidence of his first cup, Vinnie's slanderous joke that Lyons always add a pinch of bicarbonate of soda before waitresses carry the pots from the kitchen might have some basis in fact. Having stirred it, Harry looks around for a moment. He is anxious to return undisturbed to his volume of poems. He notes that the plump fair-haired soldier with the Transport Corps flashes has left the table and he is not displeased.

Which serious-minded youth having bought all the re-commended books (and seen them set aside for despatch) would hesitate to spend the residual cash on one more personal purchase? Which almost seventeen-year-old with literary interests would wish to be disturbed with witless questions while glancing through a new book of poems? The book is new to Harry. The writer is very much alive and has Tony Acker's approval as a socialist.

Harry refills his cup and indulges himself with a second spoonful of sugar. As he stirs his tea, he looks across the expanse of the large circular table to the place setting used by the soldier. He is proud – almost smug – that Stephen Spender's poems must have riveted his attention. How else could he have failed to hear the intrusive soldier asking somebody else for a light? That he *had* done so is obvious, for Harry observes a cigarette still smouldering in the ashtray. Harry smiles. A little sadly. There seems to him much that needs changing in a world where two young men so differently preoccupied can share a table. One avid for the clean skies and exciting foothills of Spender's opening landscapes and the other – a product of superficial schooling – reduced to passing the afternoon by pestering strangers with questions about the time.

Spender is propped up between the remains of a cold toasted tea-cake and the hot water jug. Harry reads on and is comforted that neither sirens nor gunfire are unlikely to disrupt the exciting skyline of pylons and factories. It is precisely as he begins a poem starting *O Young Men O Young Comrades*, that he is conscious of the hair at the back of his neck beginning to rise with excitement. All is as Hopalong Bentham suggested it should be in a literary appreciation class. Spender is delivering the genuine goods. The man has an irritating tendency to omit unnecessary definite articles but Harry skims on. He reaches the phrase that enjoins readers to *sleep with friend on hill*. It can hardly be a wartime shortage of paper or type – Harry reasons – that causes the poet to avoid making the phrase *girl-friend*. Harry gulps with the realisation that Spender's line might equally apply to doing it with Joe. He rereads the line to be certain he has not misunderstood and – as he does so – is aware of a prickling not only at the back of his neck. Something is crawling steadily up his legs.

He can think of nothing to do other than to concentrate on Spender. This becomes increasingly impracticable as what are indubitably human hands grip first his knees and then his thighs. There is a moment's respite before a mouth and nose begin to nuzzle at the flies of his grey flannels. Harry sits sweating with embarrassment and iced in terror. How – he wonders – would any passing waitress react were he to inform her that he is being indecently assaulted under a tablecloth while the three-piece orchestra plays selections from Ivor Novello? Harry notes that – despite the continuous nuzzling – he is not getting an erection. Some comfort but not much.

He closes his book and flutters his fingers in the air to attract attention so that he may pay his bill immediately. The waitress who served his tea passes with a loaded tray at shoulder height. She smiles affably but does not pause.

Harry clenches his fists and drums them on the table with frustration. The nuzzling stops and he hopes the unseen ravisher might have given him up as impotent. He edges his chair back with the thought that perhaps by standing up he may prompt the waitress to give him his bill, fearing he may be about to slink away without paying. Before he can begin to rise, the foraging hands become visible. They lift the ground-level hem of the table-cloth between Harry's feet. It rises like the ruched curtain at a cinema before the main film begins. It is not, however, Laurence Olivier or Margaret Lockwood who appears but the perspiring features of the very much undeparted blond soldier. He rests his chin between Harry's knees.

–You looking for a naughty boy, then? Me name's Alfie.

Harry shoves back his chair, caring little whether the soldier might collapse into the position of a Muslim at prayer.

–You should be ashamed of yourself. Only animals do it without being properly introduced to the person they're making love to. Just count yourself lucky, Alfie. I happen to be a socialist. Otherwise, I'd report you to the management.

*

No sooner has Vinnie rested the leatherette shopping bag against the wheel of a bookstall than a squadron of blowflies foregathers. She shoos them away using her hands as fans. Stooping breathlessly, she folds over the top of the bag to protect both her own supper of lamb's liver and some offal for her cats. The September afternoon is warmer than she had anticipated and she has no doubt that her nose is already shining again like the rivers of England. As she straightens up she pulls lorgnettes from the pocket of her threadbare bargaining coat and is about to open them. She clucks her tongue at this latest instance of forgetfulness. Although she would rather not admit it to any of the family, Vinnie is surer by the day that her lapses result from living with only de Montfort and Lackland for company. Repocketing her lorgnettes, she consoles herself with the thought that she has not yet begun to invent sustained conversations with her tabby cats. She assumes her little-old-lady-in-lavender-and-lace simper. This – or so she hopes – will distract the stallholder while she rummages for her cheap Woolworth's spectacles and balances them on the tip of her wrinkled nose.

–Lovely day, isn't it? Would you mind if I ferret around for a few minutes? I'm after something a bit different. A present for my grandson. He's off to college next week.

–You won't find much here for a scholar, Duchess. You're welcome to nose around all the same.

Common sense suggests to Vinnie that she should not linger among the battered copies of Victorian poets. She bases this not so much on whether the broken cloth and card covers might enclose works that Harry would dismiss as uninteresting, as on the possibility that the reading list with which he'd set off in the morning might have included Longfellow or Hood.

She clatters along to the far end of the stall. It is a passable imitation of a poor septuagenarian seeking something she cannot quite afford. More privately, Vinnie has every hope that whatever she does buy will leave sufficient small change in her purse for a couple of portions of the excellent bread pudding that is always on offer in the window of the cake shop by the bus stop.

A collection of, perhaps, a dozen volumes is separated from the rest by a piece of card torn from an old shoe-box. The card is marked HISTORY in red crayon. Vinnie pauses and calls to mind nights when seven-year-old Harry had shared her bed and she had read him to sleep with accounts of poor little Arthur blinded on the orders of King John or another Arthur extracting a sword from the rock. With the tip of her index finger, she eases aside

131

Macaulay's *Lays of Ancient Rome* as unsuitable. She herself had tested Harry on Horatio holding the bridge before he had won a speech prize. Her estimate of her grandson suggests that he would not be pleased to be reminded of his recent childhood.

Her finger passes, then returns to, a holly-green cloth cover with faded gilt lettering. She admires a Tudor rose stamped into the spine: *Lives of the Bachelor Kings of England*. She opens Agnes Strickland's book and chuckles as she translates the Latin numerals on the title page. Printed – she calculates – near on ten years before Lavinia Leonora Cosser was born in Kingston Walk. She warms to the illustration of William Rufus in a pose that could remind Harry of the cigarette cards he once collected. It stirs in her own mind something once recounted to her when the family had been on a church outing to the New Forest during the Great War. She leafs through the yellowing pages disfigured, here and there, by brown marks not dissimilar to the graveyard spots on the backs of her own hands. Without success, she tries again to recollect just what it was a young curate had said with a knowing smile about Rufus. Something connected with the monks' hatred of the king because he wouldn't marry for appearance's sake?

Something about a fondness for the Saxon peasants with whom he sided against the monks? Vinnie shrugs at her own failure to remember and places the book in the only clear space on the stall. A breeze flicks the pages back and Rufus is revealed once more with his crown of gold oak leaves.

–How much are you going to rob me for this one?

–Couple of bob to you, my dear. Been on my hands since the Town Hall copped it in the blitz.

Vinnie picks among the small change in her purse. She pushes aside a threepenny bit that will come in useful when she makes the Christmas pudding.

–Here's hoping yer grandson don't start getting any fancy ideas from this one, eh, ma?

132

–He's got enough already to give him brain fever. And he gets his nose from my husband's family. We know what that means, if you don't. The Welsh girls where he's going'll have to keep their hands on their ha'pennies. . .

The book weighs down her bag so that Vinnie is glad of a rest every dozen steps. She pretends an interest in junk stalls and in the polished mounds of apples until, at last, she reaches a striped awning that protects home-made cakes and pies from the late afternoon sun. She wavers for a moment, torn between a blackberry and apple tart and the bread pudding. As she peers at the display case, a monstrous gale never experienced before in England sucks in Vinnie Plimsoll and the window glass and the contents of the shop before expelling all in a chaos of timber, glass and limbs across the cobbles of the open market.

★

–Giving yourself a spot of Dutch courage before the great adventure?

Harry is not displeased to hear Cliff's voice at his shoulder and turns to greet his godfather with a smile. Cliff – he is sure – will not rush home to phone the news round the family that he has just met his under-age nephew in a bar.

–I'd love to buy you a drink, Uncle Cliff. Fact is I'm just back from buying books. There's just about my bus fare left. . .

–Forget it, Harry. Forget it. I'll buy you one if it's not going to lead to another dust-up with your Mum and Dad.

Cliff indicates to the woman who produces a whisky for him from under the bar that she should set up another shandy for Harry. He then leads his nephew to a well-stained table near the Refreshment Room door. Harry finds the bare table top reassuring. No predatory sex maniac is lurking beneath it.

–So what brings you here on a Thursday afternoon, Uncle Cliff?

–About time we made it Cliff, I'd say. Me? Oh, just happen to have been over this way finishing a bit of Council business, you know. Popped in for a quick one. The car's outside. I'll drop you home. Now . . . tell me, Harry . . . are you going to be able to manage on the money front?

–Of course. I may have more than enough. Father's doubling my pocket money so I'll have ample.

–Reconciled at last to the fact that it's time you struck out on your own, are they? I may not say much, Harry, but I've got eyes and ears. What're you going to do with any cash you've got left over? Spend it on the girls or invest it in the Post Office?

–No. I'll see how it goes for a couple of months then I may write and tell Father I don't need as much.

–Bit of a change of tune, isn't it? The dutiful son after all, eh?

–Not a bit. I'll be telling them in my own way that I can stand on my own two bloody feet. Ruddy feet. Sorry.

–I wonder if that's what your mother will tell the rest of the family, though?

–She can do as she pleases. I'll know the truth.

Cliff laughs and Harry puts down his drink.

–So what's so funny in that, then?

–You sound so much like her. We've always said you've got her flair for colour and style. Sounds like you've got a slice of her tongue too. . .

–Not her cruelty, I should hope.

–She's a plain spoken Scot, I grant you. Cruel, though. . . ?

–She laughs at my friends and pokes fun at any ideas I've ever voiced.

–I think you bewilder her a bit. Might do a bit of good if you brought home a college pal or two at Christmas time. Knowing your mother, it might be best if they can tell a fish-fork from a winkle-pin though. . .

–That's just it. They may laugh at such things where I'm going. Miners' sons, I mean. There's more important issues to them than table manners. . .

Cliff stops circling the base of his glass through the wet rings on the table top. He leans back a little and

134

tilts his head slightly to look at Harry along the sides of his nose. Harry wonders whether the grandfather he does not remember considered people in this particular way. It does not occur to him that Cliff's habit is one he himself might be developing.

–And to you, Harry? I've been thinking for some time we may have more than a bit of youthful rebellion in the family. You've got the socialist bug, boy, and no mistake. Now how on earth can you know the way the working class lives? Your father would never let you do a newsround, so I doubt if you've seen more than the outside of a council house in your life.

–You're wrong there. I have. I've been to Joe's . . . he's . . . well, someone I've been doing Messenger Service duty with. I do know what it's like to be poor.

–No need to get heated. We've no slums in this borough so you can calm down.

–No, I can't. As a councillor you shouldn't, either. If it isn't a slum to cover the table with a newspaper and eat vegetable stew because you can't afford meat, I don't know what is. And they have to sell their butter coupons to families like ours so they can buy more margarine.

–So you've been doing some research at your friend's . . . Joe, was it? What's his father's wages going on? Betting slips passed behind the barber's chair? Where's the parents each night? At the corner pub with the little ones crouched on the kerb over a bag of chips?

–No, Cliff, they are not. Joe's mother's got bronchitis. And I'll tell you another thing. We both know the name of their noble ruddy doctor but I'll protect the guilty by not mentioning it. . .

–Go on. Why not?

–Well, it's Dawkinson and you play golf with him. Noble, hypocritical Dr Dawkinson stands at the bottom of the stairs in that street and demands his fee before he'll go up to treat a patient. That's shocking and you know it.

–The man has to live.

135

–And so does Joe's mum. Cliff, it's all got to change. It really has.

–And who's going to pay for it?

–We all must. And Dawkinson can swop his golf clubs for a stethoscope.

–Are you coming back to teach in the borough, Harry?

–Are you warning me off or doing the well-known family trick of changing the subject?

–More than that, boy. No threats. I was just thinking . . . two or three years and I might have my own nephew standing against me for a seat on the Council.

–Not a chance. This place won't change. I bet you'll soon tame the blokes coming back from the Forces. Nothing personal, Uncle Cliff, but this place is all sewn up. Harding and I have talked about it. The Council's packed with builders like you . . . and estate agents. It's bad enough that I'll have a County loan round my neck for five years, without having to come back here . . . even if Aunt Winifred's friend would let me in one of her schools. . .

–You've got the gift of the gab right enough. Being a bit unfair, though. Even we Conservative has-beens could do with a few new ideas. . .

–You'll not get them from me. But you could pass on a word to the dear Alderman about the way they treat young teachers at County Hall. D'you know . . . Noreen's cousin's just finished at college. When she went for an interview those arrogant buggers – sorry – those arrogant wretches didn't even invite her to sit down. We're God Almighty Middlesex, young woman, so just you know your place. That's going to change, too.

–Harry . . . Harry. You really are a thin-skinned generation. Mightn't it just have been an oversight?

–I'll give you that. But can you explain this? She wanted to work in the north of the county in a state school specialising in History and Art. They kept her waiting until four days before term starts. Know what she heard this morning?

136

–I'm about to learn.

–You are, Cliff. Dear Miss Humby – now these are almost the very words – you have been allocated to Teddington and should take up your duties at St Fishface's Junior School where you will teach all subjects during your probationary year.

–We all have to make some compromises, Harry. We have to deal with the world as it is. . .

–Not me, Cliff. And not Noreen's cousin. She wrote back and told them she's not a box of eggs to be allocated somewhere.

Cliff looks at his watch and decides against another drink. Harry's recklessness disturbs him, yet there are moments as he listens to his nephew when he almost envies this teenager for whom choices are open that could never even have been glimpsed by young ex-servicemen returning from the Flanders slime. He understands more clearly how bewildered his own elder brother and sister-in-law must be by the sudden intrusion of Harry's assertions. Neither of them had glimpsed lives very different from their own through the camaraderie of service life. A few years in colonial Kenya could have offered only a chapter of petrified history. No preparation for coping with a youth who would mature in the third quarter of the century.

–So where do you propose to go then, Harry? Not thinking of sticking in South Wales I should hope? Teachers are falling over one another there, I should imagine. They won't hang out the banners for a middle-class refugee like you. . .

–Me? Middle-class?

–What else do you think you are? Don't kid yourself, my boy. . .

–I don't consider myself to be any class.

–It's a quick answer. Not sure you've thought it through, though. . .

–There'll be opportunities. Anyway. To answer your question I'm not sure where I want to go. It's got to be somewhere by myself. Promise you won't laugh?

–I would if you told me you don't want to teach at all. If you said you'd changed your mind and wanted to join me in the business after all. . .

–Sorry, Cliff, but . . . no. I know you're considerate to your workers and play Father Christmas for their kids each year but . . . thanks all the same. My secret dream – it may change – but at present it's Australia.

Cliff replaces his glass on the table. He gets up and Harry follows, anxious to hear his uncle's reply.

As they are crossing the station forecourt Cliff speaks with careful indifference. To Harry it is disappointing that his uncle appears to give more attention to selecting his car keys than hearing more of his plans.

–Surely Africa could be more exciting . . . colourful. . .

–I'm not a missionary. Anyway all those exclusive clubs for civil servants would remind me of garden parties – Conservative ones – in the sun. . .

–And of your Mum and Dad's tales, no doubt. . .

–Perhaps. Australia's got sunshine, too. No servants and a master-race, either. . .

–I couldn't argue about that, but I'd be amazed if it turned out to be the Utopia you seem to be expecting.

When they have settled into the comfort of Cliff's Austin sedan, Harry winds down his window to enjoy the last of the September sunshine. Cliff switches on the ignition but, before he lets in the clutch, turns to his nephew. He speaks in a tone that conjures up for Harry the sadness in Vinnie's voice as she calls *Goodbye* when he closes her gate and is about to cycle home.

–See here, Harry. I don't object to your well-intentioned socialism. Time might change your mind on that but . . . on the other matter . . . if you ever did think of coming into. . . What the bloody hell was that?

The explosion is unheralded and prolonged. Cliff turns off the engine and they both jump from the car, leaving the doors open. Passers-by have stopped to stare north-east in the direction of Brentford and the munitions factories that border the Great West Road. Harry wonders whether they may both have been so absorbed in discussion that neither heard the air-raid warning. Cliff dismisses this and suggests there might have been some accident, perhaps at Brentford Gas Works. No further explosion follows. Having watched the plume of smoke drift towards them in the south-west breeze, they return to the car. Around them strangers with puzzled faces remain chatting.

★

The nails and screws are of assorted sizes. It is the kind of collection amassed in most households. As he runs his eye a second time along the picture rails, John Plimsoll winces. It is not the crazy angles at which they have been hammered in that pains him. To him screws call for a gimlet and a screwdriver, not three wallops from the nearest hammer or even the sole of a stout shoe. Margaret shows little interest in such details. She leaves her husband in the middle of the small dank bedroom and tweaks aside the canvas. Having reassured herself there is indeed a cupboard door in the entirely obscured wall she steps back.
–I'd noticed your mother becoming a little forgetful these past few years, but I'd not supposed she was becoming downright eccentric.
–Don't say that, my dear. You know she's always been interested in history and things. Obviously she was about to start work on some kind of a family tree. . .
–You wouldn't say that was a little presumptuous, John? Yours is an honest enough family, I grant you. Not exactly the Anglo-Saxon kings or William of Normandy, though. . .
–Now I come to look at the thing, it seems to be more to do with the here and now than historical.
Margaret joins him and they study something that is more the design for a work than anything completed. Nor is there any rough sketch on the work table which overflows with hanks of tapestry wool in two dozen shades. The floor is littered with old copies of *Picture Post* and brown wrapping paper weighed down by a

139

pair of dressmaker's shears. But no rough sketch ruled to scale. Nor has the immense canvas been divided into workable rectangles. Dozens of needlework pins secure photographs and silhouettes to the projected tapestry in a seemingly random way. To some of these a strand of wool has been pinned, perhaps an aide-memoire, which would have reminded Vinnie of the shade she would ultimately have used. Near the centre – but not exactly – is the one complete fragment. A sun the size of a football and the colour of a blood orange dominates all that surrounds it. Both Margaret and John find their eyes return to this again and again. Margaret feels whatever else might have been the effect of the finished work, this sun would have thrown the whole out of balance. She hesitates to say this, surmising that her husband would not wish to hear further criticism of his mother. John himself finds the sun deeply worrying. It is to him some terrible explosion of blood illuminating them all. He finds a momentary comfort in following the outlines of the clouds surrounding it. Vinnie has cut them from brown paper. They are reminiscent of clouds which illustrate a child's fairy tale or the carefree cumulus of a Walt Disney cartoon. He removes his glasses to blow his nose vehemently. For the third time since they entered the cottage, he wipes his eyes. Margaret ignores this and waits until he has repocketed his handkerchief before speaking.

–Would you not agree that one or two of the details are a little odd, to say the least?

–How so?

–Had that old photo of you in tennis clothes been stuck against a boat, I could have understood. She seems to have confused you with Cliff. Why should he be stuck against a boat? He wouldn't know what to do with the thing. And is that supposed to be Winifred next to him? She's as tall as I am and that little outline only comes up to Cliff's shoulder. . .

–I expect they were just stuck in temporarily. She must have been designing this for months. Where are *you*, my dear?

–Well, if you can't use your eyes. I know she's never cared for me but . . . over there in the top right-hand corner. . .

–How extraordinary. Why are you sitting on all those heads? You haven't worn that frock since we sailed for Mombasa. I expect she couldn't find a more recent snap. Wonder why she didn't ask. Where's Harry?

Margaret doesn't bother to reply. She presumes John is again asking a needless question. It is becoming increasingly noticeable that he does so as a substitute for conversation with strangers or when he is ill-at-ease. It is obvious to Margaret that her husband must have noticed the collage Vinnie has devised to represent Harry. If for no other reason than its indelicacy, John cannot have overlooked it. Walter Cosser in an armchair with a pint pot in one hand and a red flag in the other is a witticism with which Margaret can concur. Harry – or more exactly Harry's head – pinned to a youthful male body not even concealed in a swimming costume seems to her – at third assessment – downright disgusting.

–This is hardly a moment to speak ill of the dead, but I do have to say, John, that your mother appears to have been attracted by the seamier side of life. . .

–Now, now, Margaret I'll not have that. We can't know whether she intended to weave in a fig leaf. . .

–That's as maybe. What are we to make of his hands clutching those two heads as though he wishes to squash them together. . . ?

–Well, one of them could perhaps be Maureen or Noreen or whatever that young nurse is called. . .

–Vinnie didn't guess as much about that young person as I happen to have seen with my own eyes. And just what are we to make of that other silhouette with a strand of rust wool pinned to its forehead? Who else has Master Harry been bringing over here on the sly?

–Search me, my dear. You see more of him than I do.

–That wouldn't be difficult, John. So, what are we to do about this? Take it down and burn it?

–Let's not be too hasty. The cottage doesn't have to be cleared for another week. Did you pick up that letter for old Walter?

–Naturally. I shall see it's posted to him.

*

Margaret McCawdie Plimsoll touches her eyelids with a grey liner and surveys the result without displeasure. Although she has, for more than a quarter of a century, made it plain she has no wish to be disturbed as she dresses, she is quite certain John will tap on the door of her bedroom. She has laid out his best white shirt. Beside it she has left two ties from which he can choose. In one way it would delight her that he might for once be decisive. Yet should he be so, and should she next see him downstairs fully dressed, she is sure he would have chosen the inappropriate tie.

Having screwed in her opal earrings she dusts a speck or two of peach face powder from the dressing-table with the side of her smallest finger. She then scrutinises her reflection to assess – or perhaps confirm – the suitability of her dress. Margaret has never doubted that she makes the best of herself in black. It highlights that Spanish inheritance in her features and colouring still very evident after five generations. If there are any reservations made by the more discerning guests, they will focus on – or so she suspects – the wartime hair-style she has lately but not very enthusiastically adopted. To roll one's hair like some continental sausage over a velvet ribbon might make one – as Harry would say – *very with it* – but Margaret much preferred herself with her jet-black waves drawn back in a bun.

She listens to sounds from her husband's room. John clears his throat with noticeable regularity. His heavy smoking is beginning to affect his singing voice. Margaret has told him so. Often. The smoke permeates his clothes from his topcoat to his vests. She sighs. The stench of tobacco was not one of the reasons she gave for her decision to move into the spare bedroom. That might have been wounding and personal. John appeared to have accepted her stated objection to sharing a bed with someone whose sleep was becoming increasingly disturbed by tossing and turning and yelling in the dark.

Turning her head, she appraises her dress and then the wardrobe against which it hangs. As soon as Harry has left for college Margaret intends to move it into his room. Not that she thrills with anticipation at the thought of Vinnie's mahogany furniture that will replace it. With Winifred having spoken for the dining table as soon as their mother-in-law died, it had been predictable that the bedroom suite would come to John's side of the family. For Margaret, the pleasure of telling Winifred the dining table should not be referred to as Edwardian but William Morris counterbalances its loss. Margaret sighs a second time as she realises that, in other circumstances, both table and bedroom suite could eventually pass to Harry. To her, his behaviour suggests this outcome as more and more unlikely by the hour.

–The boy's an oddity.

She is a little shaken by the realisation that she has spoken aloud in an empty room. She attributes this slightly unnerving phenomenon to the strength of her feeling about Harry. A bewilderment amounting at moments – such as the moment that has just passed – to distaste. Despite promises that he will write regularly, she expects no more than a routine scrawl of commonplaces shoved in the cardboard box with his dirty washing. She accepts that there will be a weekly consignment of shirts to be scrubbed and ironed. Equally she is sure that he will respect her veto on socks. She recalls – not for the first time – her son's preposterous outburst a couple of days back. What else but common sense could have dictated her throw-in birthday present to him of a tin of deodorising talc? To have rejected it with hysterical

143

allegations of a wish to humiliate him again in public seems to Margaret to be laughable.

–Sorry to disturb you, my dear. Which of these ties do you think? The grey or black?

–You might have knocked, John. I've no wish to be surprised in my petticoat by Harry.

–I did knock. Perhaps you were still thinking of the funeral. Maybe it ought to be the black. . .

–Nonsense, John. That would make you look like an undertaker. Wear the grey. . .

–Then why on earth did you put the other one out?

–Did I? You're not going to tell me I popped a black handkerchief in your top pocket, I hope?

–No. A grey one.

–Well, there you are then. Wear the tie to match. I just hope Winifred won't indulge in one of her howling sessions in the middle of the evening. . .

–That's a risk we must take, my dear. I did ask you about cancelling this do.

–I still think we made the right decision. Life has to go on, John. We need a few new faces among the rest of us. Winifred will sit like a snivelling raven so we do need some distraction.

–Who else do we expect?

–Ask our son. All I was told was about a half dozen of his friends. I'm amazed he's that popular if he treats them as he treats us. . .

–Well, let's just hope things are about to change for the better. Nothing like leaving a good home to make him value it in the future. I'll let you get dressed. It's getting on for half past already.

Margaret slips the unbuttoned dress over her head. Its bishop's sleeves with alternate panels of figured lace and velvet convey precisely the striking appearance she intends. A plainness and simplicity that will offset Winifred's predictable fussiness. She trusts that black will not only suit the occasion but might also intimate that guests should not anticipate a rowdy evening. With luck – augmented by a casual hint here and there – the house

144

could be quiet by midnight and she will then be able to finish another chapter of *Jane Eyre*.

For a third time she picks up the posy of artificial violets to try them against the waistband of her frock. She is still in two minds about them. They had been bought at the never-very-cheap shop at the top of the hill. Nevertheless, to wear them would be a signal to Harry that his underhandedness has been forgiven. A sudden foreboding tips the balance and she replaces the posy on her dressing table. A dash of lilac or heliotrope or violet has been a joke in John's family for years. Margaret recalls the origin. Alice Dowsett. To have telegrammed news of Vinnie's funeral to the woman had been further proof of Harry's furtiveness. Margaret is intuitively certain Harry has also invited her to his farewell party.

★

After twenty-five minutes at the bus stop, Jeremy Bentham considers whether he should not go home and send on the book by post. He eases discomfort in his leg by resting on the low brick wall of a cottage garden. His wife – he is forced to concede – argued with commonsense that if he wished to sacrifice an evening crossing the borough on not very dependable transport, he could at least be doing so for a star pupil with an Open Scholarship. Bentham admits ruefully – as he has already done once – that Harry Plimsoll is not even a convincing pupil. More of an actor. Always ready with a showman's plausibility to improvise reasons for lapses in written work. Even as he shapes this analysis Bentham knows he is being unjust and attributes this partly to an extra twinge in his ankle. He searches for a more positive assessment. Harry has always delighted in words. Whether his wider vocabulary can be accounted for by an inability to spell the most straightforward nouns and adjectives is neither here nor there. Again – Bentham begins to enthuse in his effort to balance his former harshness – the boy has always been eager to discover more in comic writing than the predictable belly laughs. Nor have the fears that Civil Defence Messenger work would impair any beginnings of scholarship been fulfilled. In some curious way, fresh enthusiasms had been undammed by night duties shared with presumably blunted minds.

He wonders whether he should mention to Harry a basic doubt about any real dedication to teaching. Indeed Jeremy Bentham is far from sure Harry will profit from two years in a teachers' factory.

Shifting a little on the garden wall, he glances along the shadows that are beginning to stretch further than the pavements onto the Hampton Court Road itself. There is no trolleybus. Not even a singing in the wires overhead indicates that there might be one approaching unseen beyond a curve in the brickwork where Bushey Park begins.

The Englishness of the scene prompts Jeremy Bentham to think of Harry's interest in poetry. He wonders whether this might outlast adolescence. Although he approves Harry's preference for Wilfred Owen to the vulgarly heroic Rupert Brooke, he has reservations about his ex-pupil's chances of penetrating the tight world of writers and writing. He concedes there may be changes once the war is over. He has, indeed, already received letters from old friends at Cambridge that suggest there may be schemes to bring ex-servicemen from very ordinary backgrounds into the universities. Bentham has no reservations about this. In every reply he has contended it can only be a good thing. Yet . . . even offered such an expanded horizon of opportunities but lacking a network of home and school support . . . Bentham winds his chocolate and cream college scarf more firmly round his neck. He recalls so many instances of literary hopes withering and writers in their mid-twenties subsiding to cynicism: promising lyricism, coarsening quickly to limericks that promote Ovaltine or Gibbs' Dentifrice. The odds against young Harry outwitting such an autumn seem slim.

A trolleybus lumbers towards Bentham through the dusk. He heaves himself up and lurches painfully on his club foot to the kerb. Once settled by the doorway, with the gift on his lap, he can relax sufficiently to wonder whether his own face appears as ashen under the dim interior light as that of the elderly Home Guard corporal opposite. Were Harry to be a fellow passenger Bentham is certain he would whisper that the man had somehow been preserved from the trenches of another war.

For no logical reason whatsoever, Bentham recalls a snippet of gossip from his undergraduate years. It certainly relates to First World War writing but scurrilous gossip is not a pastime Bentham enjoys. Quite unbidden he hears again a quiet aside and can visualise – without effort – a minimally raised eyebrow. Some quip at Wilfred Owen's expense. Something on the lines of most young officers caring for their men but Owen being in love with one or two. Gossip. Nothing in any of Owen's printed texts to support it. Bentham wonders whether there might be unprinted and unprintable fragments on a subject that had prepossessed his own forebear. It is unlikely – or so he feels – that Owen's private affections will ever be made public any more than his own progenitor's arguments.

The elderly corporal is beginning to stare at Bentham with something more than casual interest. He has the look of a well-meaning stranger about to lean forward and offer First Aid or some intrusive questions on the state of a fellow-passenger's health.

Since the pain in his calf is easing by the minute, Bentham can think of no reason for such an interest. Until he looks down. He has unconsciously been turning the brown paper parcel over and over in his lap. In that instant he connects his previous thoughts with the contents of the parcel. An impulse to ring the bell and leave the trolleybus becomes almost overwhelming. He considers walking home and sending on, instead, any other book. An eighteenth-century novel. Poems by William Morris.

A Shaw play. Anything other than *The Ballad of Reading Gaol* would be a more suitable gift for such a loner as Plimsoll.

As the trolleybus edges round the crater left by a recent doodlebug, Jeremy Bentham converts his near panic to a slightly lop-sided smile. For two reasons this broadens to a grin. First, because he has often caught Plimsoll doing a passable imitation of his smile. Secondly because he might have ballsed up the situation even more by using the school duplicator to run off one or two very liberal passages from Great-great-great-grandfather's thoughts on sexual relationships as a farewell gift for Plimsoll. To have left a spare copy for Old Garstone's secretary might have done something to cheer up a wet suburban morning. And a wet suburban mind. With difficulty Jeremy restrains himself from open laughter while the ancient corporal sits considering him with a suspicious stare.

It is as well that the advance across northern France is going smoothly again. The corporal has at the back of his eyes the enthusiasm of a minor functionary about to do a public duty and apprehend a deviant character.

★

–Did you enjoy it this time?

Sue completes her scrutiny of the patchwork quilt nearest Harding's crotch before replying. To her the whole business is messy enough without leaving tell-tale stains on her parents' bed linen.

–Well, come on Sue. Did you?

–Not as much as when we use a Durex. I just know it's all going to turn out like my mother says. . .

–You never told me you had heart-to-heart girlish chats with your mother.

–I don't, you twerp. I meant the woman always has to cope with household expenses in the end.

–What possible bearing has that got on whether you do or don't like doing it with me?

148

–Well, old sticky cock . . . if you spent fewer evenings guzzling shandy with Harry Plimsoll and stuck to lemonades we could afford Durex, couldn't we? Then we shouldn't have to finish it off outside every other time.

–Don't be prudish, Sue. What you mean is you like feeling it in you.

–It's all right. More to the point, there's less to clean up afterwards.

–Show me you love me then. Give us a kiss on me throbbing knob.

–Honestly, Paul Harding, you're downright vile at times. Have you looked at the time?

–What's time between lovers?

–Shut up and leave the poetry to Harry. For Christ's sake get dressed while I have an up and a downer in the bathroom. You know how Old Mother Plimsoll gets if she's kept waiting before she serves half a pilchard and a lettuce leaf.

–Mrs P. is a much misunderstood woman.

Sue is moving into the bathroom as she calls back to Paul across the landing.

–That's your opinion. Wouldn't it be nice if the man who proposes marrying me the day he qualifies, managed to give a quarter of the interest he shows in the ruddy Plimsoll family to his intended.

Harding is again torn by unease. He feels increasingly that Sue expects more of him than he can reasonably offer before he has completed his degree and his conscript period. He has no intention of quarrelling about the Plimsoll family or – more specifically – his friendship with Harry. Despite a perceptible divergence between Harry's enthusiasms and his own, Paul is convinced there is something more durable in their friendship than reminiscences of schooldays which a few weeks' distance and a few shandies are already beginning to distort. He tries – as he has once or twice previously – to formulate some basis for this conviction. He is sure it must include an acceptance of Harry as the younger brother he never had. Somehow the definition of their friendship would have to include a sense of protectiveness for an unworldly companion given to small deceits and fabrications as a defence against predators.

–Are you going deaf, Harding? I said, what have you bought him?

–Bought who?

–Harry, you idiot. You did promise to find something that would speed the traveller on his way.

–Shit. I left that to you, Sue.

–Might have guessed it.

Catching her image in the dressing mirror, Paul sees forgiveness in Sue's eyes. He winks and turns to face her. She accepts his wolf whistle of appraisal as a compliment to her party rig-out and tells him he should refer to her hand-knitted blue and white sweater as the Waterman's outfit, since she completed it during evenings when Paul and Harry have been out drinking. Paul – for his part – accepts the rebuke with a laugh and is privately delighted by her appearance. She wears slacks well without having the look of someone off to do shift work at a factory bench.

–Come on, Sue. You got him something, didn't you?

–I hate to quote my mother again. . .

–But you will, honey-bun. . .

–My mother's often right. You men are nothing but fourteen-year-olds in long pants.

–That makes you guilty of interfering with under-age boys.

–At times you make me feel as though I'm involved with a sewer.

–As a doctor's wife you'll confront life in the raw. Might as well get some practice in. What have you bought him?

–It was difficult, Sexy Legs. Very difficult. He's your bosom pal.

–We're not that close.

Harding – attempting to button his blue shirt and finding it more difficult to do so by the week – speaks with a twinge of unease. Sue moves towards him and pushes up his chin to help. She addresses his Adam's apple.

–That's as may be. You're his, I can tell you. Keep still and breathe in, can't you?

–How'd you mean?

–Shut up. Well . . . Noreen told me in the Ladies the last time we made up a foursome for tennis that Harry became quite sentimental about you. She was asking who he'd miss most when he goes into exile among the wild Welsh.

–Bound to be a wrench for him. Will be for me when I join up. . .

–Right. There you are. Don't choke on anything this evening or you'll have apoplexy.

–Anyway. If Plimsoll misses me it just shows someone appreciates my first-rate intellect.

–Let's hope that's all it is.

Paul pushes Sue back to arm's length and his look is one of genuine puzzlement. His face is red and he knows it. The ambiguity of her remark ignites, for him, a forgotten afternoon on the sand. He hopes the extra flush this prompts in his features will be attributable to the constriction of his thickening neck. Harry's bare shoulder against his own after swimming and Harry recoiling as though he had thoughtlessly contacted a live electric terminal.

–What's that supposed to mean? Ladies and gentlemen, I give you Sue Naylor wearing her celebrated Earth Mother look. Enigmatic and knowing. Come on, enlighten a poor unworldly medic.

–Has it ever occurred to you, Paul Thickhead, that Harry might be one of those funny men?

–Funny? He's a bit of a comedian, I'll grant you. Not quite in the Tommy Handley class but not so bad on Hopalong Bentham and others. His own Aunt Winifred, for instance.

–Perhaps you should be a vet. What I mean is could Harry be what my. . .

–Not your mother again?

–No. Not just my mother. What your parents and mine would call queer. Wanting to do it with other men. Not with girls. Do I have to draw a diagram?

151

Paul replies quickly. He needs to employ words as weapons against images rapidly surging between his own eyes and Sue's. An experimental wank with Charlie behind the fives court (but at least four autumns back), Charlie muttering smugly that he'd also been there with Harry. Noticing Harry linger after rehearsals to talk quietly with whoever it was had played Freddie Eynsford-Hill in the production of *Pygmalion*. Nothing really. Not in the same league as climbing into someone else's sleeping-bag at farm camp and being expelled. Or using your mother's make-up when she happened to be out doing war work.

–Sue. For Christ's sake. Harry's not a sex maniac. He's an only child. . .

–So are we.

–For crying out loud, let me finish. He's a bit arty. All this poetry business. You don't expect poets to behave like paratroopers do you?

–They might be less suspect if they did.

–Why don't we leave it to Noreen? She and Harry'll work things out. You'll look back on what you've just hinted at with a giggle when we have that double wedding. Let's forget it. What did you get him?

–Remember we were talking about Modern Art? Well, you two were. I went into Smiths and got him one of those new books with coloured reproductions in.

Harding – settling the waves in his hair with his fingers before slipping on his Air Training Corps forage cap – pauses. His face very straight, he looks at Sue once more through the dressing mirror.

–Which one?

–Well, I've never heard of the bloke. Thought all the dancing negroes would appeal to Harry though. Well, after all he likes jazz. Now I'm not unwrapping it, so don't ask. You can see it when we get there. What's so funny? At least I remembered to buy something. What's more, you owe me half.

–Not laughing at you. Laughing with you as Bentham would say. And I don't owe you a farthing. Just take a

look under my raincoat, will you? You might recognise
the wrapping paper.
–O, no. Sexy Legs . . . you didn't?
–Calm down. It's another one in the same series. Lots
of ladies with tits like melons on the jam tins. That
should put your mind at rest. They should point Harry
in the right direction and take his mind off me. After
all you always say my nipples would shame a new-
born kitten. Now. Are you ready or do we get there
so late we meet ourselves coming back? As *my* mother
would say?

★

Some awkwardness is involved both in the giving and
receiving of the camera. It is not a purchase handed
impersonally to Harry by a shop assistant. That his
parents have selected a camera as his going away gift
amazes and delights him. True, he does bite back a
defensive and ungracious comment already shaping in
his mouth as he unwraps the almost festive paper. A
box camera does not demand of its user any great
technical competence. The winding-on of film and the
extraction of a used spool presupposes little dexterity. So
John Plimsoll's faint surprise that his son should appear
puzzled is understandable. Possibly John does not have at
the forefront of his mind at seven thirty on this particular
evening his usual terse dismissiveness when discovering
Harry attempting any manual task.
–*Give it here will you? Give it here. You're about as practical as
a cow with a musket.*
Harry *does* remember, yet bites back an impulse to turn the
phrases against his father as an ironic question. Instead he
busies himself aiming the viewfinder successively at the
upright piano then at a street lamp outlined beyond the
orange net curtains and, finally, at the sun and moon on
the face of the grandfather clock. He hears, as he does
so, the soft rasping of flesh against flesh. John Plimsoll
is flicking his thumb against his forefinger in a way that

Harry is beginning to associate with self-consciousness and tension.

—So let's just see you make some use of the thing. You should have enough pocket money left over to let your mother and me have some inkling of this place you're going to.

—Of course, Father. This really is smashing. Thanks. . .

The regular friction of thumb against forefinger continues as father and son look at one another. Harry notes with pleasure that for the first time he can dissociate John's mannerism from an impending row. He considers whether it might be a symptom of his father's lack of assurance in facing any personal relationships at all and concludes that the prospect of a houseful of guests is accentuating John's apprehensions.

Making one more attempt to construct a Bailey bridge across a chasm that seems to widen daily, Harry decides to risk a gesture of thanks and a compliment. He rests the camera on the coffee table and throws one arm around his father's shoulder.

—Honestly, Father. I can't think of anything else I'd rather have had. Whose idea was it? Come on. Confess it was yours. . .

John breaks away and fumbles for his cigarette case.

—That's enough of that. It comes from your mother and from me. Who thought of it's neither here nor there. Have you got to wear that darned tie? Looks like an egg salad.

Harry turns away to pick up his camera.

—Well, it's too late to change now. Can't you hear Winnie in the hall?

—Aunt Winifred.

—Yes, Father.

*

The explanation that a baby-sitter had let them down does not seem entirely to satisfy Margaret. Although Jeremy Bentham cannot imagine why this should be, he is not overconcerned. His original intention — to hand Harry the book and slide away after one sherry – has been thwarted. Margaret has hemmed him into an alcove and barricaded him with a pile of snacks and the promise that another English teacher will be arriving. He nibbles unenthusiastically at a sandwich and admires a writing desk beside him. In a just world, a schoolmaster's salary would enable him to replace his own woodwormed work table with just such a pleasing piece of Regency rosewood.

As he vacillates between his remaining salmon and cucumber and his untouched tinned asparagus, Jeremy Bentham becomes conscious of Margaret Plimsoll moving in his direction while her son brandishes a camera in the middle distance to commemorate the encounter.

–Tell me, Mr Bentham, do you think there's any future at all in this poetry business?

–Forgive me, Mrs Plimsoll . . . are we talking about Auden or the Sitwells?

–Not the Sitwells, although I was reading a fascinating article about Renishaw the other night. I was talking about my son's scribblings. Maybe he's less secretive with you than he is with his parents. It wouldn't be difficult. What I have glanced at . . . odd bits left about, I mean . . . seem to be a lot of socialist rantings. All about derelict streets and underfed shop assistants. I'm sure I don't know where he gets all these unpleasant ideas from.

–Not a bad thing surely, Mrs Plimsoll, to be conscious of a world beyond our leafy suburbs, is it? We all wanted to see things changed when we were seventeen, I suspect.

–At seventeen I was trimming black hats for sailors' widows in Portsmouth, Mr Bentham. I think you're being naughty and avoiding my question. Don't you think Harry should have his mind on his books more than getting mixed up in politics? Not that we blame you, of course. . .

–The notion hadn't occurred to me. Maybe his imminent change of landscape will do wonders for him. As for the poems . . . if he never publishes a word the exercise will sharpen his perceptions of the world.

–I expect you know best. I do hope you'll have a quiet word with him before you leave. It's these books he's beginning to bring into the house. Shaw for instance. The man's an eccentric. Eats only vegetables. You're not going to pretend GBS isn't a raving socialist?

–I'm not. Do you enjoy reading, Mrs Plimsoll? Perhaps you don't have time for much other than the occasional magazine?

–You couldn't be more wrong. I'm a great reader. Dickens. Such marvellous comedy. Daniel Quilp. And Little Nell. Even now I can't read the death of Little Nell without weeping. But of course you're immune to such weakness.

–Not at all. Tears roll down my cheeks when I reread Little Nell's death. Well, we share an enjoyment of Dickens's keen observation. What about Uriah Heep and Miss Murdstone? We can still find their like even now, can't we?

Bentham wonders whether he might be going too far. He flicks a glance upwards but Margaret's attention has faltered. She seems to be listening to something or someone beyond the open sitting-room door. From the perceptible squaring of her shoulders, Bentham concludes she is displeased but intends to take no immediate action. He hears Harry's unmistakable voice through the doorway and reminds himself that he should tell his ex-pupil that few of the photographs are likely to be more than underexposed smudges in the genteel light of the sitting room.

–Well, yes. I suppose we can. You know, Mr Bentham, I don't think Harry fully realises how much of a sacrifice sending him to college is going to mean to us.

–I must have misunderstood. Didn't he tell me he has a loan from the County? You must know he has a Book Scholarship. I would have thought your own contribution wouldn't be more than apprenticing him to a solicitor. If as much.

–It may seem very little to you. We don't all come of such distinguished families as your own.

–Mrs Plimsoll, a family name can ease open the Bank Manager's door but it doesn't generate philanthropy.

–I'm sure you're right, Mr Bentham. I think I see Paul Harding over there with his young lady. Should I bring them over?

–Please don't put yourself out. I knew Harding before he lapsed into thinking a retort is merely a piece of chemical apparatus. Don't worry about me. I'm not chairbound and you do have other guests.

Harry observes his mother's too-set smile as she moves to the centre of the room. He has been explaining to Noreen that he intends to send her a weekly photograph that will summarise the landscape or person he has found most fascinating. With almost no explanation, he hands the camera to her and hurries over to Jeremy Bentham.

–How did it go, J.B.? Was she hell?

–To me, or to herself, Harry? Work that out on the train. I rather care for you calling me J.B. I must encourage your successors to do that. A little more humane than Hopalong.

–My successors? I'd never thought of them like that.

–They'll probably be even more revolutionary than you appear to be.

–Me?

–I suffered a tirade from your mother. You'd best not let her see my parting gift. The writer was also a socialist. It occurs to me – which route do you take tomorrow to this Welsh teachers' factory?

–I've never heard you sound snobby before.

–I'm not. I deplore the system. They should be part of the universities so you could get drunk with lawyers and fall in love with dentists.

–Never thought of it like that.

–Well, for Heaven's sake try thinking first in the future. Now. Which way do you go Wales?

–Slow to Reading and change to the main line there.

–I thought you might say Reading.

–Why?

–No matter. Open your present five minutes before the train pulls in and look immediately to your . . . let's think . . . to your left.

–Sounds a cross between a treasure hunt and a socialist slogan.

–It could be. Either. Or both. Or, maybe Harry, it could be a reminder to me that I should think first.

★

Having seen – not merely heard second-hand but seen – her own name among the first six on the guest list for the Mayor's Christmas Ball, Winifred is still – more than five hours later – planning her costume. It would be more accurate to state that Winifred is planning how she may obtain the necessary material without clothing coupons. That she will appear as Nell Gwynn she has long since decided. It would be uncharitable to suggest her interest in Noreen Humby is prompted by an appetite for black market coupons alone. She does not dislike the plump and slightly colourless trainee nurse who has dropped in for tea with Harry a couple of times.

Noreen watches Winifred approach with some distaste. She has observed the woman often enough to be convinced that Winifred Plimsoll is relentless in the manipulation of others. No occasion is too trivial. Even when dropping in at Winifred's for a cup of tea, guests are directed to chairs rather than allowed some haphazard choice. During the party, Winifred has apparently contented herself with badgering John Plimsoll to play the piano to no avail. Noreen suspects she herself is not being singled out for the attractiveness of her dress alone.

–Noreen dear, how are you? Did your father like that Algerian wine I sent? The grocery boy did deliver it, I hope. I gave him a packet of Woodbine but you never know with some of these lads today.

–Dad's keeping it for the night we enter Berlin, Mrs Plimsoll. He's coming later to collect me so he'll be able to thank you himself.

–Oh, good. Now you mustn't mind me saying so but you should watch that figure of yours. We can't have a dumpling marrying into the family, can we?

–I'm only just seventeen, Mrs Plimsoll. Trainee nurses soon lose their puppy fat, you know. They keep us at it in the West Middlesex. . .

–No need to tell me, dear. I was there for my operation. They removed every bit of the bedroom furniture. Not that a girl like you would know anything about such things.

–There's nothing very complicated about a hysterectomy, Mrs Plimsoll.

Winifred rests her sherry glass on a coffee table with little regard for the polished surface. She rubs her palms together briskly for Noreen has unwittingly scored a direct hit on a bunker more precious to Winifred than her cache of tinned goods and imported wines.

–Well, there was about mine, let me tell you. I'm forbidden to do housework ever again. Gardening's out of the question and so I concentrate on my social work. When you're more experienced you'll understand these things. Now let's talk about something pleasant. Does your mother like red salmon? I'm not talking about that pink muck they buy on the council estate.

–You'd have to ask her. I can't remember ever tasting it.

–You ask her for me, dear. I have a little arrangement with the lady on the bacon counter. I slip a pound note into the ration books and she looks after me. Now don't look down your nose, dear. Harry does that look. He's always on about merchant seamen risking their lives, but if I don't buy it someone else will.

Noreen at last sees a way of ending the conversation. Her distaste for Winifred has intensified to hostility and boredom. As Winifred has prattled on, Noreen has considered whether she is not, in fact, bored by the whole gathering and might have passed the evening more pleasantly with her Canadian. In her annoyance she dismisses Harry as having used her merely as a left-luggage office for his precious camera.

–Mrs Plimsoll. If you are after some more clothing coupons, why don't you say so?

–Oh, my dear. Not so loudly. True enough, your mother was kind enough to fix me up with coupons for this dreadful dust coat but I do have the Mayor's Fancy Dress Ball coming up.

–You look most distinguished in black. Couldn't you tack on a false piece to make it full length?

–Wouldn't do for Nell Gwynn, dear. I hate black. Trust old Vinnie to catch us all on the hop. Never did have any consideration for others. If she hadn't been rummaging around in that street market full of fleas and spivs she could have been here tonight. Mind you . . . she'd have been embarrassing us all with *Knees Up Mother Brown* after a couple of glasses. . .

–Mrs Plimsoll. Harry is coming over for his camera. I think he wants to take us together. Try and smile, even if you're still upset by yesterday's funeral.

*

–Will you put that ruddy toy down for a minute, H.P.? Miss Dowsett's just been saying you appear to be acting like a hired photographer at your own party.

–But you didn't agree with her, my faithful ally?

–Bit difficult to disagree.

They move out further from the kitchen door as Harry joins them. A ribbon of light spooling from between the almost closed curtains of the dining room is hardly strident enough to bring shouts of protest from neighbours. It is sufficient, however, to emphasise the clash between Alice Dowsett's purple cocktail frock and John Plimsoll's flowering runner beans. Noticing this, Harry regrets it is not daylight and that his film is only black and white. He is delighted by the prospect of a three-way conversation with Harding and the bizarre Miss Dowsett. With them, at least, he need not fear personal criticism and an outbreak of sweat that will propel him to the bathroom for another scrubbing of his armpits.

–Oh, come on, P.H. I've been round doing my social bit.
Miss Dowsett twirls her sherry glass between thumb and forefinger. Harry thinks momentarily of his father's mannerism but then – recollecting lunch in Winchester – he braces himself. Miss Dowsett is about to fire a little salvo.
–But have you been attentive to that pretty little thing? Noreen, isn't it?
–Oh, we went out last night to say our goodbyes. She's all right.
–And your poor gran scarcely cold in her grave. Shame on you H.P., you lecherous swine.
–Shut up, Harding.
–Well, dear, your frightful Aunt Winifred tells me you didn't weep once at the funeral. Can't say I noticed. Is there some unfeeling streak in you, young Harry? Not that I give a pair of dirty knickers for anything that twittering sparrow Winifred says. . .
–I'm still weeping inwardly, Miss Dowsett. It won't stop for a long time. In this house one only shows emotion about the kitchen cat. When the R.A.F. bombed that dam a couple of years ago my dear mother wept into her *Telegraph* for the poor bloody animals. Not the people.
Hearing a burst of laughter from inside the house, Alice wonders whether she should comment on the contrast between Harry's outburst and somebody's obvious enjoyment. The voice was male but not John's light tenor. She concludes it was probably one of the two visiting schoolmasters. Harding offers her a cigarette but – like Harry – she declines. Her glance lingers on the two friends. These she instantly transforms to young circumnavigators about to embark for a world as colourful as that depicted in her library books. She concedes their clothing to be somewhat more sober – if Harry's tie is discounted. It seems more appropriate to thrust her imaginative view of Harry and Paul forward a couple of centuries. She conceives of them as Nelson and his beloved Captain Hardy treading the cobbles of old Portsmouth towards the bo'sun's whistle and the Victory.

–Now listen, Harry. I speak to you as your friendly medical adviser. I think you've enjoyed having us all on. All this codswallop about a battle to the death with your parents to avoid being buried – sorry – stifled in some bank or a solicitor's office. Did you, or did you not, hear what your dear old dad said not half an hour ago?

Miss Dowsett smiles. Taking advantage of what little light there is she concentrates on Harry's response. Her mouth moves ruminatively as though trying to extract the stone from an under-ripe plum.

–Oh, we all heard that. I was ruddy amazed. And then I was terrified. . .

–Terrified? After all the nice things he said?

–Yes, I was. Terrified that anyone could manage to distort the facts like that. It was like listening to them on the wireless pretending there'd been an explosion at the Chrysler Works when we all knew it was the latest secret weapon. The one that killed Vinnie. . .

–You still haven't given me any proof, H.P.

–There isn't any that I can send you in a specimen jar. You've seen what I've been through since the beginning of the year, Harding. And then for him to stand up and waffle on about what a good thing it was that his son and heir would be miles away from Jerry's last fling. . .

–Very natural, H.P. Any father would. . .

–Very plausible, you mean. All that propaganda about travel broadening the mind and hoping it would do something for my poetry. You heard what he said about South Wales. I've told you he's petrified I'm going to be infected by young socialists but you all laughed when he joked about bringing me down to earth so Mother and he would at least understand one line in ten of what I'm writing. It's a travesty. That's the word. Vinnie would confirm it.

In the pause that follows Harry's appeal for confirmation, Harding drops his hand gently on his friend's shoulder. Miss Dowsett finishes her sherry before lifting her wrist-watch to within a hand's distance from her eyes. Conscious that there can now be no corroboration of his

162

own analysis, Harry's shoulders begin to buckle. Harding flicks his cigarette end over the garden fence.

–I *do* believe you, mate. That's to say I believe there's no other way you could cope with the past months. As your medical adviser I'd point out, yet again, that they've all – except Vinnie and Miss Dowsett here – resented your growing up. Vinnie's death won't help and it's another good reason for you to scarper. With her gone they all feel older. Bit nearer the end of the perch, eh? Sorry, Miss Dowsett. Anyway, Harry, we'll have to make sure it doesn't happen to our own kids.

–But that's a long way over the horizon for you two boys. I think you should both have jumped on your push-bikes and had a farewell weekend together in dear old Pompey.

–What would have been the point, Miss Dowsett? Harry and I see each other most days . . . as you were . . . a couple of times a week anyway.

–I've always needed one close friend, Harding. Harry shows signs of something like that too.

Although Alice Dowsett's suggestion is well-meant, Harry interprets it as intrusive. To camouflage his instant wariness, he tries to head Alice in another direction. To him the conjunction of bicycles and a shared weekend spells Joe Gibbs not Paul Harding.

–Would you like me to send you some photos of the college? It seems to be close to a river so I expect I'll be able to do some rowing.

–That's very kind, Harry. Yes, I really do feel you should have gone to Portsmouth for a weekend. Now you're out of school uniform you could have got to know one another as young men.

–But I told you, Miss Dowsett, Harry and I do know one another. We don't need to go boozing in some sailors' pub. It isn't as if either of us will be going in the Navy. And the reasons for that I couldn't possibly discuss with a lady.

–Oh, Harding, how very squeamish of you. You'll make me laugh and that's not good for the heart. I lived in Pompey for most my life, you know. I do realise there are bars for men only. Some, of course, are for officers.

Vindicated. Harry's lips do not move as he repeats the word to himself. He is glad to have trusted his instinctive wariness. Nor does he suppose Alice's drift is less plain to Harding. That he is about to reply on both their behalves Harry is in no doubt, for Harding executes a preliminary shifting of his increasing weight from one foot to the other. Harry is content to be silent.

–Sounds interesting, Miss Dowsett. If you'll excuse me a tick, I ought to pop in and find Sue.

Alice smiles, saying nothing to encourage or discourage a break-up of the trio. Silently amused at his friend's discomfort, Harry laughs. If challenged, he would not reveal that he is wondering with amusement how deeply Alice's concept of their friendship might have imprinted itself on Harding or how long it might linger.

–Why bother, Harding? Sue was chatting to Noreen. She shouldn't come to much harm unless Tony Ackers likes his women young and virginal.

–Who's Tony Ackers when he's at home?

–You'll forget the names of your patients. Ackers . . . the bloke who teaches at the orphanage. The one I met at the Sitwells' do.

–Oh, him. She'll manage. Anyway, H.P., what's your Dad given you, would you say – apart from the camera and all the codswallop?

–There are times when I think Sue would be better off without you, P.H. Do you do your psychiatrist's couch turn with her?

–Let's leave the couch out of it. Mustn't strain Miss Dowsett's heart. Seriously though. Do you go fully armed into the great offensive of life as Old Garstone used to say?

–I dunno. Well. An interest in music. Father hates jazz of course but he's good on classical. He's always dragged me to everything from oratorios to awful musical comedies.

Both Harry and Paul turn to Miss Dowsett. Her sudden gasp of breath suggests to them that she may be unwell.

164

Recalling again lunch at Winchester, Harry relaxes. Although her eyes remain closed and her head continues to nod appreciatively, he is certain she is merely indicating a wish to interject.

–Then why will your father not play for me tonight? I told him I wish to sing. How else can I pay tribute to Vinnie's memory except by letting her hear – from wherever she may be – an aria she always loved. Oh, yes. You two young bucks can't know the pleasure we had from potted operas at the end of the South Parade Pier. After we'd heard *Samson and Delilah* I bought the sheet music of *Softly Awakes My Heart*. I sang it to her every Sunday evening that summer but then your grandfather passed and saw her in the window and that was that.

–But if we could come up to date for a moment, Miss Dowsett . . . why wouldn't Harry's Dad let you sing?

–It would evoke too many memories too soon after the funeral. That's what he said. I'd say he's terrified of that wife of his. She loathes me and I wouldn't be here if it weren't for Harry's telegram. I'm hidden like a saucy postcard at the back of the family's linen cupboard.

Harding's eyes are merry with the uninvolved amusement of a bystander. Harry wonders if this dispassion may be a rehearsal for work in the dissecting lab or for performing vile operations in a field hospital no more than minutes from the Japanese lines in some Asian jungle.

–You'll be able to sing it unaccompanied for Harry in his college vacs, Miss Dowsett. Meanwhile, he's slid off the couch. I was going to ask him if his mother's just been putting on a public face tonight as well. Come on Harry. How do you see her? Some witch from a fairy tale who's missed her turning and ended up in the suburbs?

–Yes and no. I was going to say that Father's also taught me patience. Something I suppose I'll need in a classroom. He's certainly needed it with her.

–But she's a generous provider. Look at all that nosh in there. Are you hinting she's mean in private?

–Bloody mean with the emotional canteen if that's not being poetic.

165

—Being a bit bitchy. Wouldn't you say, Miss D?

—Not exactly. My conviction is that Harry will never come to terms with the former Miss Margaret McCawdie under this roof. They'll have to work out some truce. An armistice.

—So he's right to leave home?

—Oh, of course. My dear young man, the plain fact is – if you can't see what's at the end of your nose – Harry and his mother have too much in common. Not everything of course or I'd find him detestable.

—Miss Dowsett, do you realise what you've just said? I'm too like my mother?

—Indeed, Harry. Her imagination and a strong personality. Your mother's downfall is that she comes of harsh and unforgiving stock. You also have some of your father's tenderness. That will get bruised in the next couple of years, of course, and you'll learn not to give too much. Now. Do I hear the rattle of coffee cups? If I don't take something to dilute all this sherry, I shall disgrace you all once again by shinning up a lamp post on my way to the Riverview Hotel. Vinnie and I would do that often when we were younger. Not easy in a bustle and boots, I can tell you.

—We'll see you home, Miss D. Bet you could still do it.

—Don't tempt me, young Harding. Remember the strain on the heart. I have to be up early to put my best face on. Someone must go and tell old Walter Cosser the news.

*

In the shadow of a Bramley apple tree Noreen and Harry face each other. They stand holding hands distanced from their parents by a dozen Victorian villas. Harry is repeating assurances that Noreen's photograph will be prominent on the desk in his study bedroom so that, as he works each evening, the two hundred and fifty odd miles' separation will be diminished to less than the distance at present between them. Apprehensive that

166

the silence which follows may denote some misgivings, he catalogues other assurances. He has made them already but he repeats his intention to write each week and enclose photographs. He will even attempt a long-distance call on her birthday. Noreen at last responds with the hope that he will not forget to do so. He asks how she can doubt him when he is already wearing loosely round his neck her hand-knitted maroon and black scarf even though he's dubious of any entitlement to wear it until he has formally signed the college register.

Noreen kisses him lightly. He does not find this very satisfying. The kiss is no more than he would expect from Sue Naylor at Christmas. It is, in his estimation, less personal than his theatrical aunt offers on the rare occasions when she and his uncle are in London. He returns Noreen's kiss more emotionally and is perplexed that she seems not to understand why his tongue probes a tiny gap in her teeth.

She breaks from him to enquire light-heartedly how he can be sure there'll be no hospital near his college with a trainee nurse who has brighter eyes and a winsome Welsh accent. He clasps her very tightly, protesting vehemently that there'll never be any other girl in his life. She uncouples his hands with a laugh that she refuses to explain and looks back towards the front gate of Harry's house where her father and his are swopping cigarettes. It seems to Harry the moment he should press for a further reassurance about Clark the Canadian mountie. Noreen's reaction is swift.

–You've no right to ask. You're free and I'm free and we're both seventeen. If you can't trust me I shall begin to be sure you don't really think of me as a person. Just someone to fit into your poems and refer to in conversations.

–No, it's not like that.

–Well, let's just see how it goes, eh? You're always on about being a poet and different from the others and then the next minute I feel I'm being cut down into a photograph to be boasted about. Come on. I've got to be up in the morning, too.

Les Humby has sounded the hooter on his motor bike twice and they can both see – even at a distance – that he is pulling down his goggles. Protesting that he may even begin a letter to her in the train, Harry grabs Noreen's hand. They run with the first autumn wind against their faces to help unbutton the waterproof covering of Les Humby's sidecar.

★

By the roundabout Tony Ackers leans his cycle against a telephone box. The carelessness with which he does so conceals his irritation from Harry, yet intensifies it for himself. Not that he is annoyed by Harry's exuberance at the prospect of the future – which seems to have displaced any regret at leaving friends. Tony is irritated by the need to accept that his flatmate is right. There will be a space in his life once Harry has left for Wales. Throughout the summer months, pleasure at Harry's unpredictable arrival to borrow books and discuss local politics has been transformed to anticipation. Eric's jokes and warnings about the hazards of fancying such a babe as Harry Plimsoll have been refuted. Only now, at the moment of severance, can Tony accept his misery and his tetchiness is that of a lover not an acquaintance. An acquaintance would not have been wounded by the casual reception of a gift. Only a lover would hope for something more than the public smile Harry had also offered to his appalling relatives. Noticing that Harry is clutching the boxed set of Mozart's thirty-ninth symphony, Tony panics. He concedes it possible the lad is more perceptive than he has ever shown himself to be and could conceivably be about to return the gift as too lavish a gesture from anyone other than the closest friend. It might also be that Harry has no wish to be reminded of his gaffe in confusing Mozart with a popular song.

–I wanted to thank you again for everything you've done. I mean that honestly, Tony. Especially the Mozart. You weren't too bored by my family zoo, were you?

–Bored? Not at all. Fascinating to watch you at work in your own native habitat.

–All that whizzing about with the camera? You know me. Just nerves.

–Don't think any of us saw it as that. I thought you were being the well-bred lad from the nicer kind of suburb.

–Something's upset you. You always get at me when you're upset. Was it J.B.? Jeremy Bentham, I mean?

–Oh, no. Pleasant man. All the assurance one should expect from a gent destined for the Headmaster's study.

–J.B.'s not like that. He liked you, anyway. Said I could do far worse than keep in touch with a cosmopolitan person like you.

–And will you?

–I intend to. Wouldn't matter whether Bentham had recommended you.

What – Tony wonders – might Harry's reaction be if he were to suggest a visit to the wilds of West Wales at half-term? He tries to dismiss the image of a guest-house with a double bedroom but cannot do so. He concentrates instead on how many days should elapse before he sends his first letter to Harry. The proposal about a weekend could be made more easily in a letter. Not the first one. There is a growing constriction in his throat and he knows he should turn on his cycle lamps and go while he can still control the pitch of his voice. A desire to hug Harry (and risk no further contact ever) is becoming close on irrepressible.

Steadying his fingers on the grips of his handlebars, he manages to look Harry full in the face. To Tony it is essential that he poses a question which might allay one doubt he's had for some weeks.

–Harry? Tell me. Were all the important people in your life there tonight?

–Well, Uncle Cliff wasn't. Winifred's husband. She said it was the effect of my grandmother's death on him. He was

169

the closest to Vinnie, or so Winifred says.

—Yes, but what about your closest friend? Was she or he there?

—But you met Noreen. You really are in an odd mood, Tony.

There is a haste and an edginess in Harry's reply. Tony – alert to any inflection or prevarication – seizes on it.

—Not at all. I mean I'm not prying. You did seem to be making a double use of your camera. Of course you were getting ready to pop us all in your album. All of us who were there. But . . . well . . . you did seem to be hovering as if somebody else might turn up . . . or as if you were upset that whoever it was didn't arrive. . .

—But who else could there be? Harding was there from school. . .

There is more to Harry's terse defensiveness than that of a seventeen-year-old exposed to the world for the first time in the context of his family. Tony is certain of it. He pulls his cycle clips from his worsteds and folds his turn-ups. Not until he has switched on the lamps and prepared himself for instant departure is he ready to try his shot in the dark. In pre-empting his question, Harry offers himself as target.

—Tony? What is it you're after? You seem to be suggesting something but I can't understand what you're at.

—All right. Almost all the cast was there, wasn't it? School . . . family . . . girlfriend . . . even me representing your future in socialism and the arts as it were.

—Quite right. So?

Although Harry's reply is flat – almost disinterested – Tony notices an uneasy preoccupation with swirling rusty leaves as Harry stamps them with his left foot. For Tony it is the moment to release the safety catch.

—I was just wondering why there was no one from the Town Hall Messenger Service. The bloke you go cycling with sometimes? Joe Gibbs, isn't it?

It is Harry's voice that is about to slide uncertainly through octaves. He dumps the Mozart records by the phone box and thrusts both hands in his trouser pockets

170

where they mumble away inaudibly.

–Oh, Joe couldn't come. But he pushed a super cycling map of South Wales through the letter-box for me.

–I see. It was Noreen's hands you were referring to in your poem, wasn't it? You weren't thinking of Joe as well?

–What? I don't think you do see at all, Tony. Joe's a good mate of mine and if you think I'd write a poem to another bloke you must be perverted. Sorry, Tony. I didn't mean that. Honestly, I didn't.

–But you said it.

–Not the real me. It must be the excitement and four sherries. Look, I ought to go back now. But I will write. Promise. And thanks for the Mozart. Look after yourself till Christmas, eh? Forget what I said, Tony. You've got the most generous mind I know. See you.

★

–Got your ticket safe, Harry?

The platform opposite that on which John and Harry stand is packed with commuters waiting for fast trains to Victoria and Waterloo. Some in the crowd are known to John; fewer to Harry. Commonplaces about the progress of Allied troops in northern France are swopped across the intervening rails. John waves and shouts unnecessarily to a couple of men with whom he usually shares a compartment.

–Seeing the lad off to college this morning. Just waiting for the Reading train now.

A dozen pairs of younger eyes glance up from newspapers to study Harry from beneath a variety of trilbies and pork-pies. He recognises a few contemporaries from nearby streets and is puzzled to notice something related to envy in their eyes. One wishes him good luck. Having advised his son a third time that he is expected to write regularly, John concentrates on shielding his cigarette and match from the breeze.

Beyond the arches of the nineteenth-century railway bridge under which the Reading train must pass, Harry can descry the outlines of a new station begun before the war but temporarily abandoned to ragwort and dock leaves. He wonders what priority will be given to its completion in post-war development. Will the Abercrombie Plan ever be implemented, so he will be able to suggest to Joe that they carry their bikes onto a new underground line connecting the Thames Valley with Epping Forest? Joe's one reservation – Harry recalls – is that there might not be a decent country pub in Epping or some remote tributary where they would be able to swim afterwards.

As he calculates it will be three months, two weeks and four days before he sees again the old bridge which he has crossed so often with his parents and with Vinnie, Harry hears his father shouting a second time in the direction of some cronies on the opposite platform. John's public jauntiness is unpredictable. Without waiting for any reply, he turns and is addressing his son, who is caught quite unaware.

–I said, are you listening to me, Harry? All this day-dreaming'll never do in a schoolroom. Now, are you with me?

–I'm listening, Father.

But Harry's attention is minimal. He hopes his visual concentration on the bridge will be mistaken for interest in the green, electric caterpillar that is inching along the tracks towards them. From where he stands, John Plimsoll cannot suspect that his son's glance is fixed above the weathered arches on a pair of bare forearms and a freckled face that rest on the parapet. The delivery bike is invisible yet Harry is certain Joe is perched on the saddle. He is equally sure that Joe will wave an exaggerated goodbye.

As the driver's cabin of the Reading train draws level with the Plimsolls, Harry ignores it and smiles in recognition of his friend's thumbs up.

–Now just hear what I say, Harry. Don't go getting yourself mixed up with any loose women. You don't want a Smoker, so this carriage'll do. In you get. Don't forget what I said about women. Watch out for those Welshmen, oo. Don't want you bringing back more of all this darned socialist twaddle.

-Father, please. We gave my school blazer to the salvage men last week. I could just as easily be going into the Army, now couldn't I?

-All right. All right. No need to start all that again. Just watch out for those colliery boys, that's all I'm saying. They're drinkers. We can do without alcoholics in the family.

The window of the compartment pulled down to its fullest extent, Harry has an uninterrupted view of Joe above and beyond his father's head. To Harry's left, the guard is waving a green flag vigorously. Joe imitates this in a crazy mime. Harry waves back as he replies to his father.

-But surely, Walter Cosser's an alcoholic, isn't he, Father?

-Less of your lip. Someone you know on the bridge?

-A good friend of mine. Another Messenger boy.

-A schoolmate, eh?

-No. He delivers Winifred's groceries. And ours.

-And he's a good friend?

-Yes, Father. And a very close one indeed. See you at Christmas.

John Plimsoll does not turn away immediately. He stands in open-mouthed bewilderment, quite unaware that Joe has blown his son a kiss. Since the train is gathering speed, John supposes the kiss Harry blows in return is directed at himself. This gesture doubles his confusion and he remains, oscillating his *Daily Express* like a metronome, until the guard's van has swung beyond the allotments and the iron footbridge.

Harry faces the oncoming landscape with his back pushed firmly into a corner by the window. It is, at first, too familiar to interest him and he ignores children in a recreation ground playing Hunt the Nazis. As a potential poet, he gives priority to his feelings on leaving his birthplace for rather longer than a fortnight's holiday. He puts excitement foremost, together with anticipation. While the train moves smoothly beyond gravel pits and towards the beechwoods of the upper Thames, Harry

173

feels he should revise these priorities. He's a sense o
regret at leaving Joe. He'd like to think it is matched by hi
regret that he'll not see Noreen until December. It isn't
though it might have been had she bothered to come t
the station.

★

The thumping is incessant. Harry reasons that if it wer
the guard he would also shout that he needs to inspect th
ticket. It is obvious someone's need of the toilet is greate
than his own. Harry gets up from the closed lavatory
seat on which he has been sitting for all of ten minutes
He inspects his reflection in the cracked mirror. A
impulsively as he once discarded his pork-pie hat, he nov
removes Winifred Plimsoll's gift. It is not the ostentatio
of wearing gold that he dislikes but the symbol itself. H
wonders why she should have chosen to fritter howeve
much the tie-pin had cost without at least offering him
preference. A plain gold bar might have been acceptable
but a running fox? Harry unclips the pin and thrusts it int
the top pocket of his sports jacket.
–So sorry to have kept you waiting.
It's the form of words he has been taught to use. The
mean nothing to him and the army corporal knows it.
–And about bloody time. Civvies first from now on, is it
Roll on the Far East if this is how things are going to be in
Blighty.
Harry knows he must return to the compartment. Eve
there, scrunched in his corner and watching a distan
haze of rain covering Swindon, he will feel less expose
and vulnerable than when clinging to the bar across
corridor window. He is convinced he will always asso
ciate Reading with loneliness and apprehension. All th
picnicking spots and the cycling landmarks of the middl
Thames Valley had fallen behind too quickly. Even afte
Staines, while chatting to the foreign and very privat
woman who had joined him, the miles had passed easily
But then she had dragged her kit-bag into the corrido

with an odd comment about Reading Gaol. Something
to do with it being a memorial to British stupidity and
cruelty. Yet at least – talking to her – he had not felt alone
among strangers.

The old man is still asleep in his corner of the compartment. Harry forces a smile at the old woman who smiles
and nods back. He knows them to be a miner and his
wife returning to the Rhondda and he reproaches himself.
These are the very people any socialist should be proud to
know. The truth of this is incontravertible, yet Harry has
to admit it in no way dispels his sense of being an outsider.
He wonders if the fault lies unknown in himself. Is it their
accent when speaking to him or their asides in Welsh that
hang like a sheet of plate glass between the two sides of
the compartment? His dismay at seeing no other students
join the train at Reading increases his discomfort. The
possibility that he is travelling on the wrong day occurs
to him and he pulls his diary from an inside pocket. As he
flicks over the leaves he senses that his palms have begun
to sweat.

-Bit nervous, is it? First time away from home like?

-Yes. Well, as a matter of fact, it is.

-You'll like Cardiff. Or is it to be Swansea Uni for
you?

-Neither. I'm going on further. To be a teacher.

-Training Coll, is it? That's nice. You'll like the Welsh.
Harsh tongues and gentle hearts we always say.

-Can I ask you something? Do you all talk politics
a lot?

-Hush now. Don't wake my Emrys. It's nothing but
old politics from cornflakes to cocoa time with him.
You'll have heard of the miners' strike even in London,
 suppose? Bad business that was. Never be peace in the
Rhondda until every pit is nationalised.

-Nationalised?

-That's right. Owned by us all it means. After the war it'll
come, and that won't be long, eh? The news is good, isn't
t, eh? You'll be sleeping in your beds again. No more old
tube train shelters now.

–Well I'm not from London itself. But you've had bac
raids, too.

–Something terrible over Cardiff Docks and all along
the Gower. Nothing to worry about where you're going
though. No pits there, neither.

Emrys stirs and yawns. Harry – who wishes he knew ever
the elementary arguments for and against nationalising
the mines – seeks some way of disengaging himself from
the discussion which he suspects will develop. In fairness
to himself he might also have recognised that much ha
already battered his eyes and ears since he waved good
bye to Joe and John. This might equally have contributed
to his decision to close his eyes and mull over the journey
so far.

–Sounds as though I'll enjoy it, then. Sorry if I'm not much
company. As a matter of fact I had to be up very early so
I'll doze for a little while.

–A party last night, too, was it?

–That, too. Would you wake me up when we cross into
Wales? I shall want to see everything then.

–Don't think we've got border guards out watching fo
you, do you? We've had seven hundred years to forgive
the English, you know. I'll wake you at Cardiff when we
get off. Ready for your snack now, Emrys?

★

The compartment empties at Swansea, leaving Harry to
recover from the impact of the coastal plain across
which the train has passed. A succession of image
continues to assail him. He stares at the platforms o
Swansea station but sour rows of miners' cottages ris
in terraces on scarred hillsides to interpose themselve
between him and placards advertising local cinemas. I
he turns to concentrate on the upholstery of the sea
opposite, the fabric becomes obliterated by monstrou
slag tips like hills of excrement marking the entranc
to each valley. In ninety minutes the green dreams c
boyhood have been stripped from him. Feeling nakedl

unprepared, he waits to meet contemporaries who have been reared in the seemingly endless desolation of this century-old war. He closes his eyes. What old Emrys from the Rhondda referred to as the pit-head winding gear revolves against his retina, turning on and on in a dark parody of the Big Wheel at a fair. Feeling close to nausea, Harry wonders whether his reaction can – in a tiny way – be comparable with Wilfred Owen's when first confronted with the battlefields of France. Not that there are corpses lying grotesquely by the ugly chapels and unwelcoming bars. He opens his eyes and glances through the corridor windows to check an impression he had been too moved to record with precision. The faces of those who scurry through the rain are indeed colourless. It is as though not one passer-by ever enjoyed a private moment to climb the hilltops and wander among the sparse clumps of heather and gorse. Harry cannot comprehend an existence that alternates between an underground shift and a bar in a dim street where it is always night.

-Get in by here, Gwyn. No one in this compartment. Oh, sorry. Anyone sitting with you?

-No. They all got out at Swansea.

-Fair enough. Hey, come on, Gwyn, you have that corner. I'm going to stretch out on here and get a bit of a kip like. Blind bloody drunk and legless I was last night, man. Stands to reason though. Off to Training Coll's a good excuse. Fair do's.

The tall yet already burly youth whose heavy brogues and cords are resting along the seat where Emrys and his wife ate sandwiches watches Harry as he speaks. Nothing indicates any relationship between the two young Welshmen but Harry guesses them to be more than chance acquaintances who have met at the Swansea ticket barrier. That they will be fellow students he doesn't doubt. Being outnumbered two to one, Harry feels increasingly ill at ease. A certainty that he is expected to say something augments his discomfort. As Harding would say – it is time to assess the stranger and his intentions.

177

–I do sympathise. We had a bit of a get-together at home
last night. My head was like a drum of dancing nails all
the way from Reading to Newport.
–Oh, from England is it? What you doing here, then?
Home on leave visiting your poor Welsh cousins, eh?
–Leave? I'm not in the Forces. I suspect we all might be
making for the same place.
–Well shit a brick, Gwyn. No one told me we were going
to meet English gentlemen.

There has been no evidence from the far end of the
seat on which Harry sits that Gwyn has been listening
to the conversation. He explodes with laughter at his
companion's crack about the English but still does not
turn from studying an advertisement for cheap holidays
in Ilfracombe. The speaker waves one hand dismissively
at Gwyn and continues.

–Ignore that bugger. My cousin Gwyn. Always a moody
sod. Back in our valley he calls himself the brilliant lazy
fucker. Brilliant he may be. Lazy he is but as for fucking
I have my doubts.
–Just piss off, Meredith. Watch your language in front of
your betters, eh?

Inadvisedly Harry ventures a light-hearted observation
that he's sure Meredith was just joking and that as
students they'll all be equal. Gwyn turns and Harry sees
his face for the first time. The skin is fair and lightly
freckled. The hair is rusty rather than ginger. Curls rusty
as coils of wire scattered on the concrete floors of disused
factories between Port Talbot and Bridgend. Gwyn folds
his arms as – for the first time – he speaks directly to
Harry.

–I'm no better than he is. How could I be? Born
three houses away from each other we were and within
a couple of weeks. I was meaning you when I referred to
our betters.
–Me?
–You . . . doing us the favour of coming to a Welsh
college in your Harris tweeds and your Van Heusen
collars. Wouldn't they have you in England, then?

178

Within the sneer and the irony there is something embedded that puzzles Harry. Since Gwyn is waiting for an answer he has neither time to pinpoint it nor guess at a cause.

–Matter of fact, you're quite wrong. . .

–Not *actually*?

–No. *Actually* I haven't got a bowler hat or an old school tie in my case. What have you got? Leek sandwiches for your tea?

–Ten points. Well said, cockney. Take no bloody notice of Gwyn. He's ratty 'cos he's nervous. You want to see him biting his nails past his elbows in the changing room before playing for the School Fifteen.

–Shut your clanging manhole, Meredith. I'm waiting to hear why the gentleman isn't favouring one of the London colleges with his presence.

–Simple. I left it too late to apply. And I am at an English college. You'll find we're evacuated to yours. Since I'm going to have to put up with you and you're going to have to cope with me you might as well know my name is Harry Plimsoll.

He speaks cautiously – picking his way from word to word as though tiptoeing through a minefield. One unconsidered syllable, Harry is sure, will detonate a further maiming onslaught from Gwyn. Both Welshmen have listened to him with curiosity and Harry wonders if he is, maybe, the first English voice they've heard other than on the Movietone News and the Home Service.

Meredith surreptitiously extracts a harmonica from the open breast pocket of his dyed battledress tunic. It occurs to Harry that the rich royal blue might have been selected to highlight blond streaks in Meredith's hair. Gwyn sits motionless weighing not only what Harry has said but also his choice of words. Before commenting he clears his throat and pulls a cigarette – a bit battered – from an almost empty pack. Before lighting it he glances at the No Smoking sign and then at Harry who refuses to be drawn.

–So. A second invasion by the bloody English, is it?

–Some invasion. More like a raiding party of a couple of dozen.

–No problem, then. Just so long as you remember this is our countryside, mate, and we own it. You don't.

–I'd need to be a moron to forget it with you around.

–Well said, Harry. Fair do's, Gwyn. He's got the cockney spirit. Give it a rest, eh?

–I'm bloody watching you, Meredith. If you want to start puffing into that mouth organ of yours, boy, you can bugger off into the corridor. Anyway, Mr Plimsoll might not. . .

–Harry will do.

–Watch that patronising drawl and I might even learn to call you Harry. What's all this Plimsoll lark, eh? A direct descendant of the M.P. who limited loading on the freighters, no doubt?

–That was a long time ago. Since then we've had two County Aldermen and a founder member of the Communist Party. And there's been space for some ordinary people between. Me for instance.

–Very impressive, eh, Meredith? Was Sam Plimsoll a cockney in tweeds, too?

–No. West Country. I heard the name came from Plum. But I don't speak with one in my mouth. And I don't have a lump of alum in here, either.

–Do we detect an attempt at irony, Meredith? Tell us, Henry – sorry – tell us, Harry. Isn't it plimsolls we put on for rugger practice? That's what you'd call them. Here we call them gym daps.

–That's right.

–So I might call you Daps.

–Call me what you like. I shall bounce back. Rubber does.

The train leaves the outer suburbs of Swansea and continues west. The tracks follow a narrow coastal plain and Harry – if he wishes to follow the landscape as it softens towards distant hills – is forced to look between Meredith and Gwyn. They can all hear endless choruses being sung in the next compartment. Both the words and the melodies are unknown to Harry but Meredith is soon humming softly and Gwyn's fingers tap out the rhythm on his elbow.

–They say there's concerts on Friday night at the college, Harry. You'll be able to entertain us with a few songs of the blitz, eh?

–Sorry. I don't sing. But you're Welsh so I shall have to content myself with listening to you, Gwyn.

Gwyn concedes the point and smiles. Harry notes a pleasing dimple in both cheeks which compensate somewhat for discoloured and uneven teeth. Meredith has no interest in what is clearly becoming a duel. Plainly, singing in the next compartment is becoming less resistible to him as chorus succeeds chorus. His hangover forgotten, he yawns once more before jack-knifing to his feet. Peering between pre-war advertisements for Hovis bread and holidays at Tenby, he combs his hair in the mirror. This lengthy routine is observed in silence by Harry and Gwyn. First, Meredith exposes all he can glimpse of his left profile. Almost satisfied, he pulls his head back and studies himself full-face. The spectators infer that something is amiss when Meredith restarts the combing routine. While this continues Gwyn turns to Harry and – for the first time – recruits him as an ally against his cousin.

–Don't suppose you realise this has been your chance to meet a rising star, Daps. We shall both be slogging it out in the classrooms when Meredith Rees has his name in lights. He's going to teach Hollywood a thing or two. Stand aside Sinatra, your time is up.

Meredith says nothing until his hair-styling has been completed and he has moved to the compartment door-frame. Improvising a microphone by extending his harmonica in his right hand he sings a very passable chorus of *Night and Day*. Anticipating that Gwyn will interject with something discouraging, Meredith breaks in mid-phrase.

–Since you two pseudo-intellectuals are happy as pigs in shit snarling at each other, I shall leave you to it. When you've discovered the world's not turned any faster for all your long words maybe you'll consider joining the peasants next door.

181

Without a breath pause he resumes *Night and Day* from the phrase at which he had broken off. Cheers which filter through the wall seconds later suggest his reception is enthusiastic. For the remainder of their journey, Meredith's distant harmonica orchestrates Gwyn's and Harry's conversation. Harry is less immediately concerned with words than with food. His lunch is still untouched. He opens the large cake tin that his mother has packed. There is no need for him to glance to his right to be aware that Gwyn is watching with a grudging interest.

–I was too devastated by the . . . the whole industrial landscape across Glamorganshire to eat anything. Look. There are two pasties. Would you like one?

–We can afford to eat.

–For Christ's sake. My father hasn't got shares in a coal mine. Do you want a pasty or don't you?

–If it makes you feel less guilty . . . O.K. Got meat in, has it?

–Yes . . . It . . . Has. And I can remember as a child having to eat the cat's fish done up in parsley sauce when my grandmother arrived unexpectedly at lunchtime.

Gwyn – in mid-mouthful – cannot answer. He does manage an infuriating smirk to signify his delight in riling Harry. The tomato he was about to be offered is lobbed rather than passed. He catches it effortlessly and acknowledges Harry's gesture with a twitch of his eyebrow. Harry finds this more disturbing than anything Gwyn has said or could ever say. It more than resembles a habit Joe Gibbs is developing.

–Gwyn. Can you understand I don't think I've ever been as horrified as I was an hour ago when we were passing the openings to the valleys. It was worse than seeing people dragged out of the rubble after a doodlebug.

–Good to know you've got feelings, boyo.

–That's right. I bloody have. What's more, the misery I saw there began a hundred years ago. How old are you?

–Seventeen three weeks ago.

–Same as me. That all began generations before we were born. So stop attacking me as if I'm solely responsible.

–Very good. Shall we sing a hymn now or later?

The exhaustion of seven hours' travelling begins to register on Harry. He acknowledges to himself that his slight headache might also be attributable to his leaving party. Not bothering to reply to Gwyn he turns to the window.

The engine of the train disappears as the tracks curve to the right. They are turning, at last, away from the coastline into a river estuary. There is now more blue than grey in the sky and the mid-afternoon sun dazzles Harry a little. Not enough to obscure the broad and tranquil valley. Immediately to his left between the rail tracks and the shore, gulls swoop in squadrons over the reddish sand. Nearer still, apple trees in neat gardens are bowed under the weight of green and pink fruit. The slag tips have given place to low hills on the further shore. Curious sheep – or so Harry thinks them – nibble lush pasture on the lower slopes. When he notices small craft bobbing by the nearer shore Harry relaxes. They are something in a fresh landscape to which he can relate. The estuary of the Towy might be only a minor cousin to the Thames but it evinces in Harry Plimsoll a sense of coming home.

The warmth of the afternoon pervades the compartment and he pulls off his sports jacket before turning again to stare at the sheep.

–Odd sheep you've got here in Wales. Black faces and white bodies.

Gwyn – licking the last of the pasty crumbs from his fingers – gets up and moves to join Harry on the opposite seat. They both peer into the sunlight.

–Stands to reason, Daps. Been down the pits, see? Heard of pit ponies, haven't you? And pit canaries? Well those are our pit sheep. They're off shift now and having their wash in the Towy. Must wash up after a shift, see? Just like our brothers and dads.

–Now pull the other leg, Gwyn. I tied Big Ben on it.

–Not suggesting I'd have you on, are you? Me, a plain lad from the valleys?

–Course not. The tutor from my college who interviewed me said all you Welsh students are just like simple Greek shepherds. That's why I asked about the sheep.

While Harry settles his head back in the upholstery and concentrates on keeping his eyes open, Gwyn lights another Woodbine and sucks at it nervously. Harry is interested to note a bluish translucent quality in Gwyn's teeth and wonders what Harding might diagnose. He senses Gwyn is waiting for him to look up. When he does so Gwyn smiles with a shyness that astounds Harry.

–Haven't upset you or anything have I, Daps?

–That would take ten Welshmen. Perhaps five of you. You shouldn't be taken in by the clothes and the accent you know. It's not been all Little Lord Fauntleroy.

–You mean the raids, eh? These doodlebugs and living in shelters?

–Not really. Tell you another time. Anyway Cardiff and Swansea seem to have copped it round the docks.

–Hitler could have done us a bit of a favour. If there's any money left we might have some decent towns in Wales, too. If we can get a Labour government there'll be pithead baths for my Da and Lord Treorchy can find his bloody profits elsewhere.

–Ever thought of going on to be a politician, Gwyn?

–Wouldn't be a bad idea. You need nerve though, Daps. Someone to have confidence in you. It's a teacher first for me, boy. Give me time to get the coal dust out of my throat. Ever met a socialist before, Daps?

–My father warned me about people like you.

They both laugh. Gwyn reaches for his cigarette packet and offers the last one. Harry waves it away.

–You don't drink either, Daps?

–A bit. I hate whisky. . .

–Nice to be able to afford it.

–Will you bloody let me finish?

–Sorry, sir.

–Shut your – what was it? – yes. Shut your clanging manhole. I was going to say I like shandy. And cider.

–You've had your last for a month or two, my old cockney sparrow. At this college they send you down if you're caught going into a pub.
–More of your Welsh irony?
–Honest to God, man. The place we're going to's a puritan fortress. All hot gospels and cold showers. Hold on.

Harry's image of the two years before him begins to crumble at the edges. Dr Jocelyn Camford, he realises, might not be as typical of the staff as he had supposed. He takes a rather negative comfort in contemplating a whirlwind of work and routine that will allow him no respite during which he might regret the absence of Joe. And of Noreen, of course.

Having closed the compartment door, Gwyn returns and leans forward confidentially.

–Didn't bring a bike with you by any chance?
–In the guard's van.
–Great stuff. Ten points, Daps. My racer's in there, too. Now we could pedal out over the hills and find ourselves a quiet pint. Just the two of us.
–We could if I wanted to.
–Well don't bother if you don't want to, you ungracious sod.
–What I'm trying to say is that I haven't come hundreds of miles to allow others to make decisions for me. It isn't personal.
–So what you want me to do, Daps? Kneel on the fucking floor and plead with you?

Harry laughs. Gwyn – nonplussed by this reaction – becomes very white around the mouth. His eyes become darker than chestnuts and he is clearly angered. Noting all this, Harry lets his own eyes laugh and drops his hands open onto the seat and signify concession.

–Gwyn, the floor's bloody filthy. Kneeling on it wouldn't come any easier to you than it would to me. Yes, of course I'll come with you for a drink, any time you like. While they're having their midnight prayers preferably.
–Well, thank Christ that's settled. Now we can get on with the arguing.

–We shan't get far. I've been counting the stations. We'll be slowing down in another few minutes.

–Have to continue elsewhere then. You might look for a room near mine.

–Or you might just fight your way to be next to mine.

–You're an arrogant sod.

–And you're a Welsh one.

–Just trying to get you used to being a socialist, Daps. You won't have many of those in the sunny south.

–And you might just be looking at one. Time to get our cases down.

–And there was I thinking it was all gallant Greer Garson and noble Leslie Howard. These middle-class films don't give a true picture of the struggle in the suburbs, do they?

–How right you are, Gwyn. We've had to dig up the orchard for vegetables. And the servant problem is hell at present. Mind you we still manage a dry sherry at six thirty, so . . . if you ever happen to be cycling past the lodge gates. . .

With his back to Gwyn Harry tugs down his case from the luggage rack. The train is now slowing so that Gwyn's open laughter overrides both the sound of the engine and singing from the next compartment.

Meredith reappears to collect his valise and a carrier bag. He looks at Gwyn but speaks to Harry.

–Didn't think you'd share the joke with me. Not that I'm prying, like. Anyway, cockney Harry, you seem to have cheered old moody bollocks up. Never heard laughter like that from our Gwyn since his great-grannie scalded her tits in the porridge. Long time ago that. Gwyn here was thirteen and still thought his cock was to piss through. See you both up at the monastery.

Swinging his carrier bag over his shoulder, Meredith leaves Harry and Gwyn looking at each other. They both shrug as Meredith passes along the corridor to conduct a chorus which Harry is sure has been sung three times since the train left Swansea. Gwyn whistles the tune as he tugs a navy-blue knitted pullover down onto his shoulders. He then pokes Harry lightly on the chest with his forefinger and suggests they should both prepare for battle. He has to repeat both the gesture and the words, for Harry – staring at Gwyn's disarranged hair – sees Joe waking beside him on a stretcher in a schoolroom. When he does reply his voice is husky.

–Why not?

He turns quickly away from Gwyn and edges round to lower the window strap so that he can look out of the window unobserved. It would not be convincing to explain the flush he knows is rising from his neck as no more than the exertion of pulling down a case on an unusually warm September afternoon. As doors open along the length of the train and students hop onto the platform a new cacophony begins in Harry's head. An opening line from Wilfred Owen runs through his mind. *It seemed that out of battle I escaped*. Leaving home had not been an escape. Merely a cease-fire. The conversation he has just had with Gwyn resembles a target practice more than a friendly discussion. Like arguments with Harding but sharper. More satisfying. He looks forward to others during the autumn months. Yet, even as he surveys the platform, brighter than a garden fete with scarves and blazers of the two colleges, Harry is overwhelmed by excitement at the prospect of a challenging or perhaps hazardous friendship with Gwyn. Plainly the rust-haired Welshman will be more than a replacement for Harding. Pressed against the woodwork of the door Harry is conscious of two simultaneous developments. Gwyn's head thrusting through his pullover superimposes itself on Joe's remembered smile and stubbornly refuses to fade. Secondly – and with an equal stubbornness – Harry's cock is rising.

–Stop dreaming of fish and chips, Daps, and get the bloody door open.

Glad of the need for diversionary action, Harry tugs the catch first right then left. It will not turn.

–Damn thing's stuck.

–Give us a go, then. We'll be off to Pembroke Dock in half a tick.

–I'll do it, I tell you.

–Our plucky little Londoner will see us through, is it?

–Shut your mocking Welsh gob and I'll do it.

The catch will not budge.

–Move that useless arse of yours and let a wing three-quarter have a go on the outside at the same time.

Gwyn crouches on the inside of the door with the back of his head thrust against Harry's thigh. Harry swallows and refuses to think of anything other than getting the door open. He knows the skin on his fingers must soon become broken and bloody but refuses to allow Gwyn to claim success alone. Both of them are gasping for breath as the catch yields.

–Some things are easier when there's two having a go, see? Bit of Anglo-Welsh co-operation.

–Sure you don't mean Welsh-English?

–I do, too, but we can argue that later. That packet by there – is it yours?

–Christ. A book from my English master. . .

–Read it yet?

–Not even looked at it. Come on.

And they saunter along to sort out their cycles from the heap by the guard's van. Harry touches Gwyn's arm.

–Hey, Gwyn? Over there. What the hell are they by the river? Giant tortoises come to welcome us from the hills?

–Ignorant cockney bugger. Coracles. Still use 'em for fishing down here.

–You're having me on again. Coracles are from the Stone Age.

–You've come to a primitive nation, Harry. Quick to anger we are. Quick to knock back a pint. In the valleys they say we're quick to give affection. Something I don't know much about yet.

–Doesn't sound much different from Londoners.

–Don't you believe it. You're a hard and heartless lot.

–Maybe you've met an exception.

188

–If I have, I'll take some convincing. That's yours, then? Trust the suburbs to have fancy green bodywork.

–So what? Green's my colour. Spring . . . being young . . . it's a socialist colour, too.

–Oh, bugger the symbolism. Has it got three speeds that work?

–Course they bloody work.

–They'll need to round here, Daps. We've plenty of hills to climb in the next two years.

–We?

–See here, Daps, are you going to start arguing again?

–Not about that.

–That's settled, then. Maybe we'll even find other things we both like doing, too.

–Maybe. Why not?

FORTHCOMING FROM
THIRD HOUSE (PUBLISHERS)

September 1989

THE FREEZER COUNTER

an anthology of stories by gay men, edited by David Rees and Peter Robins.

Peter Burton, Michael Carson, Martin Foreman, Patrick Gale, Ian Hutson, Charles Lambert, Joe Mills, David Nott, Edwin Preece, Dave Royle, Tom Wakefield and Gregory Woods are among the contributors.

ISBN 1 870188 11 X   £4.95/$8.95

THE COLOUR OF HIS HAIR

a novel by David Rees about two gay teenagers whose relationship leads to persecution at school, and a surprising denouement ten years later.

'a first-class writer of enormous significance'

Time Out

ISBN 1 870188 10 1   £4.50/$8.50

ALSO PUBLISHED BY
THIRD HOUSE

ORANGES AND LEMONS

an anthology of stories by gay men, edited by David Rees and Peter Robins.

Keith Adamson, Paul Davies, Paul Gurney, James McVey, Chris Payne and Philip Ridley are among the contributors.

'a deeper exploration of the gay experience than could be squeezed into a novel of thrice the length.'

Gay Times

ISBN 1 870188 00 4   £3.95/$7.50

PHOBIA PHOBIA

a second book of gay cartoons by David Shenton, creator of the irrepressible *Controlled Hysteria*.

'a unique combination of artistic facility, perceptive social observation, and a sense of the absurd.'

City Limits

ISBN 1 870188 08 X   £3.95/$7.50